I0451382

The Shades of Us Trilogy Book 3

Crimson Vows

ABBY FARNSWORTH

This is a work of fiction. Names, characters, places, and incidents are products of the author's imagination or are used fictitiously and are not to be construed as real. Any resemblance to actual events, locations, organizations, or persons, living or dead, is entirely coincidental.

World Castle Publishing, LLC
Pensacola, Florida
Copyright © Abby Farnsworth 2023
Hardback ISBN: 9798386816537
Paperback ISBN: 9781960076441
eBook ISBN: 9781960076458
First Edition World Castle Publishing, LLC, March 27, 2023
http://www.worldcastlepublishing.com
Licensing Notes
All rights reserved. No part of this book may be used or reproduced in any manner whatsoever without written permission, except in the case of brief quotations embodied in articles and reviews.
Cover: Karen Fuller
Editor: Karen Fuller

Table of Contents

Dedication

To Anne and all the girls who wish with all their hearts, they could live forever.

"Some say the world will end in fire,
Some say in ice.
From what I've tasted of desire
I hold with those who favor fire.
But if it had to perish twice,
I think I know enough of hate
To say that for destruction ice
Is also great
And would suffice."

"Fire and Ice" by Robert Frost

Acknowledgments

Thank you so much to Karen Fuller, not only for doing her usual work but also for editing this novel! I have no idea what I'd do without you. Thank you to World Castle Publishing and everyone there who provides me with endless support. You all are amazing. Of course, thank you to Nicole for making sure I don't crumble and Alyssa for checking in on me every week. There are so many more I'd like to include on this list, but if I do, it would go on forever. So thank you to those I haven't mentioned but know you matter to me.

To all of my readers, thank you. Those of you who have stuck with me since the beginning are some of the best people I know. And my new readers, I owe you a special thank you for deciding to explore this wonderful world. I hope you all love the final installment of The Shades of Us Trilogy.

To the girl who finds comfort in the idea of forever and the prospect of eternal life, I see you. In fact, I was you. From Twilight to The Vampire Diaries, I'm with you all the way. I hope Crimson Vows makes you smile and helps you get through those hard days when all you want is to be swept away by an immortal.

Prologue

It was a star-filled night, the kind where all you wanted to do was admire the light that caused a silver glimmer to glide over the earth. Savannah was lit up by the brightness of the downtown activity, as well as the full moon and shining stars. I rested with my hands against the balcony railing while my black hair flowed around my shoulders like silk in the night air. From the penthouse view, everything was more magical. There was romance in the existence of such a beautiful night.

My red dress flowed down around my knees in a soft, crimson river. I felt it brush against my skin as the air around me stirred with the promise of rain. I didn't mind the glim weather; in fact, I enjoyed the fresh smell it brought to the atmosphere.

Albert had just finished reading a bedtime story to Penny. It was a fairytale about a lost princess who had been found and rescued by a magical king. I laughed the first time I heard him tell it. Penny was one-year-old. She was walking, and her first word had been 'Mamma.' I could hardly believe how much she had grown. Some days, I didn't want to acknowledge it.

Sometimes when I looked at her, all I saw was the same petrified baby girl in the arms of Albert's deranged, homicidal sister, Hazel. We had rescued Penny from a party full of blood-hungry beasts, and now we were the only billionaire vampire parents in the world. It was a rather strange reality. She didn't know the difference, though. At one-year-old, her most pressing concern was how much chocolate she could convince Albert to give her. He typically folded under the pressure of her sky-blue eyes, so she normally got as much as she wanted.

She loved her aunts and uncles, too. Whenever Albert and I went out, Nina and Anya would keep her. Roy and Arthur provided her with hours of entertainment. I rarely left her with anyone else. Nina and Anya were great babysitters. Unlike Albert's sister, they weren't interested in sucking the life out of my daughter.

Penny had lived in London, Savannah, and the French countryside for a few short months. Albert was determined to take her everywhere. We had been back in Georgia for a few weeks, but I hoped to convince Albert to stay for a while. Penny wouldn't grow up the way I had. She was a 21st-century baby. But I wanted her to see what normal felt like because she was human. Normal no longer meant much to me. I had lost the very sensation when I had been turned. But I wanted it to mean something to her. Penny deserved to have friends and do basic, human things like go to school. After all, we could only hide the details about us from her for so long.

I loved Savannah, but I didn't really care where we decided to raise Penny as long as it was far away from Hazel. I couldn't think of a long enough distance between us that would make me comfortable. Living on the same planet seemed too close. At least we weren't currently on the same continent. That's why I wanted to leave France. It was too close to London. I wasn't against taking Penny to a cabin in the middle of Colorado for the next eighteen years, but Albert didn't approve of that plan.

"She's asleep," Albert whispered.

I hadn't heard him come onto the balcony. He was quiet and old enough that his senses were better than mine. He never scared me, though. His voice was always gentle when he spoke to me. Penny and I were the only two people he was ever soft with.

I smiled. "You always get her to go down easily."

He placed his hands on my hips. "Well, my stories are better."

I laughed. "Mhmm."

Albert gently turned me around so that I was facing him. My back was against the cool, damp railing of the balcony. Small rain drops were falling upon us as he placed a soft kiss on my lips. The air was frigid, but it made me feel alive. I was very much dead — we both were — but moments like this made me forget I was a vampire. When he kissed me, it was as if we were truly alive. Maybe immortality wasn't all that different. After all, there was a part of me that felt human. Albert made me look forward to eternity rather than dread it.

His curly hair was wet from the rain, and water dripped from his cheeks. Albert was the most handsome man I had ever seen and almost otherworldly perfect. I could feel my own raven hair plastered to my neck. My dress was wet, and my porcelain skin was starting to glow. There were some perks to being a vampire. One was that I looked really good in the rain. "I love you, Anne," he whispered.

I kissed him back. "I love you, too."

He gently stroked my cheek. "I can't wait to marry you, Anne Emerson."

In that moment, I felt more happiness than I had once believed possible. Our souls would be permanently tied so that no power on earth or beyond could ever separate us. Albert would be all mine, forever.

Albert leaned forward to gently place his lips against my own. "You're going to be my wife. Whether in life or death, I'll make sure you know I'm yours for as long as this universe lasts and then even after that."

I bit my lip as a small, contented sigh escaped my mouth. "Always, Albert. Always."

With supernatural speed, he stood and wrapped me in his arms. I wrapped my hands in his thick, curly hair as his fingers traced my hips. I breathed in as much of him as I could. The taste of his lips was everything I had ever wanted. Albert was going to be my happily ever after.

Chapter One
SOMETHING OLD

"I like that one," Nina said.

This was the fifth wedding dress I had tried on. It was a high-necked Victorian wedding gown with lace accents and three layers of satin skirts. I loved the way the fabric brushed against my skin. It was tight around my chest with a see-through lace area that began at my collarbone and went up to my neck. Beneath the floor-length skirt, I wore a pair of white kitten heels. It really was the most beautiful dress so far. It matched the bright diamond in my engagement ring.

"I think it's the one," I replied.

"Yay!" Nina squealed.

Her silky-smooth black hair fell against her shoulders as she stood to examine the fabric buttons on the back of my dress. Henna tattoos accented her hands from her recent trip back to India. Her eyelashes fluttered as she concentrated. I felt her agile hands running against the satin. I could see her bright red lips form a smile in the mirror.

Anya, who was holding Penny, walked into the room. "He's going to love it. Seriously, it's pretty much perfect."

Penny, not understanding why we were all so focused on a bunch of dresses, protested for her aunt's attention. Anya turned back to her with a bottle in hand.

Albert had organized an impromptu wedding dress gallery in the ballroom of his–our–fortress. It was an expensive apartment building where the coven lived, but sometimes it felt safer than Buckingham Palace. The place was like a mansion. We lived in the penthouse sweet but had started to spend more time on the eleventh floor when Nina, Roy, Anya, and Arthur moved in. Not only did their floor include the biggest rooms, a movie theater, and a lounge, but also a gigantic, regal ballroom. The whole place was magnificent. But even with the gorgeous chandeliers in the ballroom, my favorite was still the warm, dimly-lit library that spiraled up from the tenth floor all the way up to a private section in our penthouse suite.

"Where's Albert?" I asked.

"Probably out doing bachelor things," Roy replied.

We all turned toward the door. Roy and Arthur were both standing inside with amused looks on their faces. I rolled my eyes, and Anya gave them an irritated look.

"You're not supposed to be in here!" Nina said.

Roy walked over to give her a kiss. "Relax, love. I just

came to witness the excitement for a few moments. Now I can
see it's not nearly as enjoyable as I'd imagined."

Arthur looked at Anya. "When we get married, there's
no way we're doing it like this."

Anya laughed. "I know."

I giggled. "Oh, get over it. A few hours in dress clothes
won't kill you."

"It's not that —," Anya replied.

"It's everything else," Arthur added as he motioned to
the hundreds of ruby roses hanging from the ceiling.

There had to be at least two hundred candles in
the room. They glimmered in the large space like stars at
twilight. Perhaps it was a little extravagant. But with Albert,
I would have expected nothing less. The floors were shined
and sparkly. Crimson curtains covered the windows. They
were the same color as my lips. Almost everything in sight
was white or red. It was the perfect location for a traditional
English wedding.

"Well," I giggled, "Albert does like to be...passionate
about everything he does."

Roy and Arthur smirked, and Nina rolled her eyes at
them. Anya tried to hide her amused expression; I couldn't
hold back the grin that spread across my face. This was the
happiest we had been in a while.

"Time for our dresses," Nina said.

Anya motioned to the door. "Time for you guys to go."

Arthur grabbed Roy's elbow as he began pulling him away. "Good luck."

Nina helped me out of my wedding dress before walking away. I slipped on a black skirt and red top before taking Penny and sitting down in one of the white, cushioned chairs. Anya smiled before walking off to follow Nina in search of bridesmaid dresses.

Penny leaned back against me as I brushed her blond curls out of her face. Her big blue eyes were glancing around the room in curiosity. Penny looked like a pretty bird about to soar through the sky. Her brightness was so beautiful. She was still sucking on her bottle as I pulled her back to cradle her against my chest. Penny was the baby I had thought that I would never have. After dying and becoming a vampire at seventeen, I had given up on the idea of a child. Those few decades had been hard. But now it all made sense. My little girl had transformed my immortal life.

Penny closed her eyes and drifted off to sleep. I took the bottle from her hands and placed a tiny kiss on her forehead. Her heartbeat was gorgeous. I could sit for hours and just listen to it. Everything about her amazed me. When we first adopted her, I was afraid she wouldn't be able to live in a vampire household. After all, it didn't feel natural. But now she was thriving and was the most beautiful baby I had ever seen. Penny was my little princess.

"What about this?" Nina asked.

She and Anya were wearing matching long, velvet, ruby dresses. They had high-neck tops with wavy bottoms and slits that reached their knees. Each of them also wore a pair of black wedge heels. Together, they looked like a pair of intimidating superstars or Victoria's Secret models. Anya's natural curls fell around her, and her brown Cherokee skin looked healthy and smooth. Her eyes were alive with excitement, and her lips parted in a huge smile. Anya always seemed happy, like light simply bloomed from her soul. Nina stood beside her, reapplying deep crimson lipstick. She was tall and elegant enough to be an actress in a Hollywood romance. Her figure was that of a truly gorgeous woman. They were more than slightly intimidating. When looking at them, I felt greatly lacking.

"What do you think?" Nina asked.

Anya lightly traced her fingers along the velvet. "I think they're lovely."

I smiled at both of them. "I do, too."

"This is so exciting!" Nina whispered in an attempt to prevent Penny from waking up.

"Hey, maybe we'll get to do it again in a couple hundred years," Anya said. "Though, definitely not with all the suffocating formality."

I shook my head, laughing. "We still have to get through tomorrow."

Chapter Two
SOMETHING NEW

It was already nine o'clock before Albert arrived home. Penny was asleep, and I was wearing my long, cotton nightgown. My current wedding-related task was laying out my jewelry for the morning. The ruby necklace Albert had given me was a must. The beautiful, mesmerizing jewel hung from a silver chain and fell just below my neck. I had worn it almost every day since he gave it to me at the start of our intense, beautifully-complicated relationship. It was the symbol of how much I meant to him. I would also wear the silver tiara Albert had given me the day we saved Penny from Hazel and her coven. It was shaped like a crown of little leaves and made me feel magical. When I wore it, I could almost pretend that I was a character from Greek mythology. Either it was that beautiful, or I had an extremely active imagination. The tiara was a family heirloom, which made it especially important. The day he gave it to me was when I realized he would be my husband. It had been a monumental night for us, changing our lives by bringing a baby into the equation. By tomorrow evening, I would be Mrs. Jefferson.

"Getting ready?" Albert whispered.

He was still wearing one of his classic suits with his brow hair in a messy collection of handsome curls. He had a knowing smirk as he watched me set the jewelry aside. Albert walked toward me and tilted my chin up to kiss my lips softly. His hard marble body pressed into mine as he wrapped his arms around my back. I felt like I was melting into him when his hands found my waist. Albert was exactly the type of man I wanted. And more importantly, he was the lover I needed.

"Where were you?" I asked.

He smiled. "That, my little dove, is a surprise."

"Tell me," I urged.

Albert shook his head. "Tomorrow."

"Please," I whispered.

He laughed. "Alright."

Albert reached into his pocket to reveal a little black box with a red bow. It was small enough to fit in the palm of my hand. He handed it to me with a smile.

"I was going to put it with your dress so you would see it before the wedding, but you might as well open it now," he said with a confident grin.

Albert loved surprising me. He took pleasure in giving me gifts that I had never imagined receiving. It was one of his favorite things to do, and now it also applied to our daughter.

He would bring her adorable dresses from France and had given her a silver necklace with real diamonds in the shape of a heart. I had insisted we save it until she was older, but he protested. She only wore it to formal events, but Albert was thrilled when he saw it on her. There were worse things than a slightly over-protective, adoring, billionaire vampire father.

When I opened the box, my eyes grew wide. I saw an emerald bracelet that seemed just the right size to be clipped onto my wrist. It was so sparkly that I could barely pull my eyes away. The bracelet was fit for a queen, literally. I had no idea where he had found it, but it was definitely old enough to belong in a historical exhibit. I was hesitant to remove it from the box.

"It's from the Regency period. I thought you'd like it," he said.

Ah, another one of Albert's recent obsessions. Having a little girl had made him obsess over all things Jane Austen. He was now making her education, which as a one-year-old, wasn't very formal, one of his top priorities. And since I had no idea what to teach the daughter of two immortal vampires, who would grow up surrounded by her supernatural family, I was letting Albert pick out her future reading material.

"It's lovely, thank you," I replied as I gently touched the little jewels.

"Of course," he answered with a satisfied smile. "I didn't know if you'd want to be alone tonight. I can go to one of the spare rooms if you'd like."

"No bachelor party?" I asked.

He laughed. "No bachelor party. I'm too old for that."

I smirked. "I'd hope so. You're pretty much ancient. I'm marrying an old man. I have no idea what's come over me."

He rolled his eyes. "You must have lost your mind somewhere in the last eighty years. I think I look good for my age."

I reached up to plant a kiss on his cheek. "You do."

Albert gently pulled his fingers through my curls. I relaxed into the way his palm cupped my face. He placed kisses along my jaw. His lips were sure and hard, not at all in a hurtful way. These were the moments that made me feel mortal. I had never dreamed I could feel bliss from only a few kisses, but he turned my world upside down. Albert gave me everything other than butterflies–these sensations were far more complex. But in the pit of my stomach, all I could feel was longing.

"You are the most beautiful woman I've ever met," he mumbled into my ear.

"I'll never get tired of hearing you tell me that," I replied.

With one last kiss on my lips, he stepped away. "I'll go now."

He was really going to leave for the night. It was

touching, but the sentiment was enough. After all, vampires didn't sleep. It's not like I needed beauty rest; I was probably just going to read. Eventually, I might finally finish all of the books in our private library. It was always better with him, though.

I reached out to grab his arm. "Stay."

Our eyes met, and a boyish grin, something I rarely ever saw, spread across his face. Albert was hardly ever so relaxed. It was ironic; the night before our wedding was the only time in weeks he had been completely carefree.

"Gladly," he replied.

"Will you get me a drink?" I asked.

"Of course, love. Anything else?" Albert asked.

"Some books," I replied with a smile on my face.

"I'll be right back," he answered.

I placed the bracelet back in the box before setting it with my other jewelry. After closing everything up, I went to put on some music. Maybe it was only nostalgia, but I preferred the record player to modern speakers. After selecting a Paul Anka record, I sat down on the bed. Suddenly, the 1950s felt a little closer.

Albert returned to the room in a pair of sweatpants with two glasses in his right hand and a stack of books in the other. After looking through the titles, I took *The Count Of Monte Cristo* from the bottom. It was an old copy with a leather binding. My familiar ribbon bookmark was still inside. It was one of my most treasured books.

"You've read that three times," Albert said.

"I like it," I replied after taking one of the glasses.

He sat the rest of the novels on the nightstand before taking one of his new Civil War books and sitting down. One day, I would try to convince him to become a professor. He could start a vampire university. Maybe not. It sounded too much like the start of a movie.

"I'm going to buy Penny the Austen collection soon. We'll start with *Pride and Prejudice*," he said.

I rolled my eyes. "She's barely one- year- old."

He flipped the page of his book. "I'll read them to her."

"And what will you do when she starts dating?" I asked.

"Have her suitors fill out an application. If they're good enough, then I'll allow them to take her on a chaperoned date," he replied.

I shook my head as he smirked at me. "Oh, you know I love you."

"And I love you," he said before wrapping his arm around me.

I cuddled close to him while continuing to scan the pages of my book. I could barely wait to be Mrs. Jefferson.

Chapter Three
SOMETHING BORROWED

"I can't find my lipstick!" Nina shouted.

She was wearing her bridesmaid dress and running around the room in a frenzy of nervousness. As always, she looked like a queen. I envied her flawless, creamy brown skin and big, doe eyes. If she hadn't already been married to Roy, I was certain there would have been many men approaching her at the reception. Nina was stunning.

"You can borrow mine," Anya replied.

Like Nina, Anya was gorgeous. Her long, elegant curls were nothing short of mesmerizing. They were what girls dreamed of having. Somehow, her appearance was both wild and free and groomed to perfection. Now, her lips were a dark red that accented her dress. She had a natural beauty that was worthy of a princess-like portrait.

"Thanks," Nina answered.

Considering the ridiculously large number of vampires

wandering around the building before the wedding, I hadn't left the penthouse. Roy, Arthur, and Albert were already out controlling the chaos. Penny was laying in her bassinet beside the chair I was temporarily grounded to. She was the only one not stressed about the upcoming events.

"How should I attach the veil?" Nina asked.

"Uh, I don't know," I replied.

Anya walked over, and they began shoving pins into my hair. My black curls were tugged and twisted as they maneuvered the long, floor-length veil into place. I hadn't chosen it. Albert had. Not that I minded; he was better at selecting those sorts of things.

Nina held a mirror up in front of me. "What do you think?"

I smiled. "It's beautiful."

The lacy veil fell around my hair like a curtain of snow and continued behind me. It was tucked just behind my tiara, so the elegant piece was still visible. The family heirloom suddenly felt a bit heavier. In a short while, I would be part of that family. I was marrying a billionaire, vampire, Victorian aristocrat—not exactly what I had imagined when I first thought about my husband as a little girl. My wedding dress was only a shade lighter than my pale skin. The vibrant red of my lips matched the ruby hanging from my neck, providing a splash of color. I looked down at the bracelet Albert had given me the night before. It still made my heart flutter. The emeralds were as bright as the juicy green of a forest after a summer rain. I felt prettier than ever before. Not only did Albert make me love him, but he also made me love myself.

Nina leaned down. "Here," she said, "something borrowed."

She handed me a pair of silver droplet earrings. They were like glittering snowflakes gleaming in the candlelight. I took them from her before clipping them in. They went along wonderfully with the rest of my jewelry.

"Thank you," I replied.

"And something blue," Anya added.

She handed me a tiny ring with a sapphire embedded into it. The ring was so small that it fit my pinky, but it was perfect. I slipped it onto my finger with a smile.

"We went to the antique store downtown. It just seemed like it was right for you," Anya said.

I smiled at both of them. "You two are awesome."

We hugged each other tightly as the sun continued to set. The hours were ticking by, and it was almost time to go. Within a few hours, I would walk down the aisle and into my new life.

~*~

I could see into the ballroom from where I was standing. Nina, Anya, and Penny were with me. My heart was racing in my chest. I hadn't realized just how scared I would be. I felt hot and heavy. It seemed as if there was pressure upon my lungs. I tried to take deep breaths to calm my nerves as the piano began to play. There was a violin, too. Leave it to Albert to hire world-class musicians. Together they made a magical sound. The ballroom was only dimly lit by candlelight, and the atmosphere felt like a fairytale. Still, I could hardly calm my ragged breath. What was I supposed to do?

"You'll do fine," Nina whispered, holding Penny in her arms.

Penny wore a little white dress with pink hearts embroidered on the bottom. She wore the necklace Albert had given her, and her curls were pulled back into a ponytail by a big, white bow. Her tiny shoes were absolutely adorable and straight out of the 19th century. She looked almost like a fancy doll. Looking into her blue eyes, I saw curiosity and interest. I wanted to carry her, but Nina would take her down for me. Out of the hundreds of people here, Penny was the only human. That in itself made me incredibly anxious. I hated having her around people I didn't know.

I held a bouquet of white roses. Their scent was sweet and almost too overwhelming. As the music changed, I focused on their aroma. I was gripping the stems so tightly that I could hardly feel anything but the pressure of my skin against them. It was silly to be so nervous, but I couldn't make the anxiety go away.

Nina and Anya smiled at me, then they left to walk down the aisle. I watched them all the way. When they got to the end, Penny reached for Albert. He gave her a light kiss on the head before handing her back to Nina. I took a deep breath — inhaling the scent of the roses — and followed after them.

I ignored the people as I walked down the aisle. So many vampires were staring at me. If I looked at them, I would feel sick. I barely knew any of these people, which made me even more anxious. All I had to do was focus on Albert. He smiled brightly as I walked toward him. When I reached the end, Anya took my bouquet. Roy and Arthur stood on the other side with Albert. I glanced over at them, and Roy winked at me. Arthur gave me a small smile. When I looked back at Albert, there was passion in his eyes.

~*~

Most of the ceremony passed in a blur. The traditional vows were repeated, and hands were held tightly. I didn't pay much attention to the words. All I was thinking about was how Albert's black-brown eyes poured into mine. I was glimpsing his soul, and he was dancing with my heart. There were so many words and vows I knew I would keep, but what I really wanted to say was, 'I do.'

Eventually, it was time. Albert watched me for what felt like a million separate little moments before smiling. I felt the weight of his hands on mine and the new, glimmering ring on my finger. My breath was heavy; I was more nervous than I had imagined possible for a vampire. My body was shaking. I was the most dangerous creature on the planet, and I was shivering in anticipation about two simple words. They would change my world and reshape my forever.

"I do," I whispered.

The clergyman looked between the two of us. "I now pronounce you husband and wife. Mr. Jefferson, you may kiss the bride."

Albert softly placed his thumb on my cheek before leaning toward me. He paused for a moment as we took in the scent of each other. This man—whom I had once thought only arrogant and immature—was my husband. There was no other person, vampire or human, I would have rather spent forever with. His lips met mine, and I suddenly knew what home felt like.

"What a lovely ceremony!" a voice shouted from the end of the room.

The space grew quiet. When I turned to look, I saw Hazel surrounded by three of her vampire-thugs. Her smooth red hair fell down around her like flames. She wore a black, Edwardian dress that looked like it belonged at a funeral. Her crimson gloves were almost the same color as her eyeshadow. Hazel looked like the vampire of people's nightmares. She would have been a wonderful match for Dracula. In fact, I wanted to ship her off to Transylvania.

A sick feeling crept up within me. I was freezing cold, and the room suddenly felt like a war zone. Fear was pounding through my chest. I took Penny from Nina and held her close. Hazel had tried to kill her, and I had no doubt she would do it again. I wouldn't let her hurt my baby girl.

"I'll take care of this. Don't worry, it'll be fine," Albert said as he stepped in front of Penny and me.

"Just another ordinary day," I mumbled. "Your homicidal sister just crashed our wedding. What could possibly go wrong?"

"Leave, Hazel," Albert said as he walked toward her.

I felt Roy and Arthur step toward me. As much as I didn't want to watch whatever was going to happen, my eyes were trained on the woman who had tried to kill my daughter. Penny laid her head on my shoulder; she had no idea what was happening. I wanted to wrap her in myself and shield her from everything, especially her crazy aunt.

Hazel threw her hands up. "I was hurt that I didn't receive an invitation."

The rest of the crowd was panicking. They all knew who Hazel was and what had happened between us. I watched as they began to disperse. The air was hot with fear. Nina and Anya stepped beside me. Together with Roy and Arthur, they formed a circle around us. With the help of supernatural speed, the whole crowd was gone within only a few seconds.

Hazel shrugged. "I guess they were in a hurry."

"Either that or they didn't feel like having a stake driven through their heart," Albert replied.

A demented smile spread over Hazel's face. "Is that the little girl? She did turn out to be a pretty thing."

Hazel's eyes met mine, and it seemed like a thousand moments passed between us. There was anger, hate, and disgust displayed on her face. She despised me, and I was completely aware of it. Never before had I witnessed so much hate in a single glance.

"You're not welcome, Hazel," Albert said in a terrifying voice.

She feigned surprise. "How rude; I am your sister. You wouldn't exclude me, would you, brother? After all, we're family."

"No, we're not," Albert replied.

The temperature in the room plummeted. Everyone froze. That was a big statement. None of us had expected him to go that far, telling her they were no longer family. She would be even more furious.

Hazel pursed her lips. "You're honestly serious about that American girl? I've tried to set you up with so many beautiful women, and you choose her? I'm insulted. You truly have lost your signature taste."

"I want you gone," Albert whispered in a harsh voice.

The men around Hazel began to spread out. I saw Nina and Anya eyeing one of them while Roy and Arthur glanced at the other two. I gripped Penny tighter in my arms. I had never before felt so threatened.

"You will go, or this won't end well," Albert said.

I had never heard him speak like this before. It was commanding. This was the voice of a king. Hazel hardly seemed fazed. She was determined to accomplish her goal, and that terrified me. I knew what she wanted and that she would not give up.

"You ruined my reputation," she said. "My coven thinks I'm weak. They assume you have control over me. By taking that worthless little child, you fractured my power."

"You have no right to speak of my daughter," Albert growled.

"She is not your daughter," Hazel hissed.

Hazel's fangs slid over her teeth as her eyes became even more filled with anger. She looked like a monster. I held Penny close and shielded her eyes, but she still started to panic. Even my little one-year-old could feel the danger. Little cries of confusion were escaping her. Penny was only a baby, but she knew something was wrong.

Suddenly, Hazel lunged at Albert. Her three bodyguards followed her lead. Nina and Anya tackled one of them to the ground. His face was covered with shock. Nina reached into her dress and grabbed a stake—she kept it for emergencies. After what had happened with James, we always wanted to be ready for conflict. They struggled for a moment, and Nina took a strong punch to the face. She took a moment to recover but managed to refocus. While Anya held him down, Nina drove the stake through his heart. I made sure Penny didn't witness it; she deserved better than the violence her homicidal aunt brought to our family.

Arthur and Roy were taking on the other two vampires. There was blood everywhere. The pretty white roses decorating the room were stained red. A pang of sadness coursed through me; it had been such a lovely wedding. Roy had shoved the first vampire against the wall. He pulled a stake from within his jacket. I watched as the vampire panicked, terror crossing his eyes. As Roy was preparing to stake him, a heart-wrenching sob echoed throughout the room. It was the kind of scream that broke the strongest hearts. Fear filled the air. A dark shadow of death descended upon the room. The sense of grief was so strong that I felt as if I could touch it. A chill ran through me as Anya's scream echoed throughout the room. The only remaining vampire in Hazel's party had just pushed a stake into Arthur's heart. Anya collapsed on the ground beside Arthur while Nina ripped into the murderer. She had fury in her eyes. I had never seen Nina filled with so much anger. In a swift stroke, she snapped his neck before thrusting her stake through his heart. Roy followed suit with the remaining attacker.

When all three vampires were dead and turning to dust on the ground, Roy and Nina joined Anya beside Arthur's form. There was hardly anything left of him. He was falling away in little gray flakes. After a few seconds, his body was nothing more than a pile of ash. Anya was grasping at the flakes of his former body while screams racked her thin form. I couldn't even look at her — it was too much. Roy was holding her against him. Nina sat there with disbelief on her face. Arthur, Anya's love — our brother — was dead. He was gone, and he wasn't coming back. Anya screamed with pain until all she could manage were wounded whispers. She sat there staring at the ashes as if she could barely believe they were his. Her eyes were glazed over as denial invaded her broken heart. It was as if the joy had vanished from her universe. Anya had always been so bright, but now she looked darker than the night sky. The energy surrounding her had become heavy and midnight black. She was shaking so violently that her body barely looked stable. I could hardly breathe. Just seeing her in so much pain made my heart break.

Penny was crying in my arms. I had to be careful not to crush her with my strength. She was so fragile. Albert's eyes were on me as I turned toward him. Hazel was on the floor with her neck snapped; it wouldn't kill her, just knock her out. In less than a second, he was by my side.

"Take Penny out of here," Albert whispered.

"What about Anya?" I asked.

He glanced over in the direction of my traumatized, distressed sister. She was having a silent panic attack. I could see it in her eyes. They were one of the worst experiences in the world. It felt like being stabbed, but unable to express the pain. Roy still held her in his arms as Nina began to gather the remaining ashes of Arthur's once-stunning form. His forever hadn't been as long as we had expected. Because of Hazel, he was gone permanently.

I could barely believe he was dead. It didn't seem possible, especially not on my wedding day. This event was supposed to have been joyful, but it had turned into a crime scene. One of my best friends had just fallen to ash. There was blood all around, and broken furniture scattered the room. Arthur had always been there for me, and now he was gone.

"I'll help Nina and Roy with Anya," he replied. "Just take Penny back upstairs."

I nodded and — still wearing my princess-like wedding dress — took my little girl out of the ballroom and back to the penthouse.

Chapter Four
SOMETHING BLUE

The moon was already high in the night sky. Stars shone in the overwhelming darkness brought on by the absence of the sun. It was a calm night. There was hardly any noise in the relaxed, beautiful city of Savannah. The air smelled of the sweet reminders of spring. I could feel the earth erupting with life. There was green everywhere. It was such a beautiful night ruined by the melancholy sadness surrounding our family.

I sat on the couch facing the balcony with only a silk nightgown covering my cold body. It wasn't the type of frigidness that could be eliminated by heat. No, it was far deeper than that. It was the cold, guilty sensation of realizing that my sister's partner—my extra brother—was dead, and it was partly my fault.

I didn't regret saving Penny from Hazel's murderous intention. She would have died if Albert and I hadn't taken her. I would have never been able to accept that. But even so,

Hazel had crashed my wedding in order to take revenge. And in turn, Arthur had ended up dead. We should have had more security or just a smaller wedding. Instead, we had thrown a party meant to be the most elaborate vampire wedding of all time. If not for the ceremony, Arthur would be alive. Instead, my sister was mourning her partner. I knew just how much they adored each other. Arthur had abandoned his position as Alpha of a werewolf pack in order to become a vampire for Anya. They would have gotten married and had a happy, immortal existence. But now, Arthur was dead, and Anya was alone.

I glanced at the little ring resting on my pinky finger they gave me before the wedding. The sapphire was so gorgeous. I couldn't look at it for very long, though. My stomach felt uneasy. The sapphire ring had been a lovely gift. It was the new token of my vampire family. But considering the tragedy that had occurred alongside it, I could no longer feel any joy at its sight. Nina, Anya, and I had chosen and loved each other for decades. Now it was different. Would Anya resent me? Would she blame me for Arthur's death? Did I hold myself at fault? I wasn't entirely sure.

Penny lay in her bassinet beside me with a bottle in her hands. Not understanding the extent of what had just occurred, she happily sucked her milk. I raised my hands to cover my face. How had this happened? It didn't seem real. Arthur had died over an hour ago, and I still hadn't heard anything. Albert was still with them. I could only imagine what was going on. Part of me wanted to be with them, and another knew that it was better if I stayed away.

Roy must have been incredibly distressed. He was now left without the brother who had been beside him his whole life. Nina was probably in shock. And Anya, I wondered just how angry she was. Everyone was devastated. But Hazel was probably joyful. I felt hate for my sister-in-law. She was one of the most disgusting beings I had ever met.

When James had died—when I had…killed him—I had barely been able to process it. He had been terrorizing the humans and had refused to control his urges. After becoming a vampire, my ex-boyfriend had lost his memories and transformed into a different person. But after I ended James's life, there had been intense guilt. I felt so much sadness and loss. The guilt had been so strong that it seemed to rip a hole in my chest. Never before had I felt such inhabilitating loss. Even though I had already begun my relationship with Albert, killing James had been painful. I still hadn't completely been able to process what I had done. There would never be a day when I wouldn't regret what had happened to him. It wasn't possible to kill a former partner and not feel a devastating loss. After all, I had loved him.

And Anya was now feeling that loss, pain, and detrimental loneliness. I didn't even know how to comfort her. I felt so much guilt surrounding the events that had led to his death. He was gone forever, and I couldn't apologize to him. Arthur had been a good man, and now he was a pile of ash. He had been kind and protected me. When I was lonely, Arthur had made me laugh. It was always his mission to make sure that I didn't feel like an awkward addition. This wasn't what he deserved.

"Anne?" Albert whispered.

He came and sat down beside me. His hand rested on my thigh. Albert's wedding ring stood out as strong, shiny, and new. I could feel his eyes upon me. There was compassion and hesitancy in his body language. I leaned in and placed my head on his chest. He let out a sigh as he wrapped his arms around me. I buried my face against him as he pulled me tightly toward his body. I slid onto his lap as I relinquished control of my being. My chest was contracting. There was so much tension within me. No matter how hard I tried to control my breathing, it was ragged and stressed.

"I know what you're thinking," he whispered into my ear.

"It's my fault," I mumbled.

He shook his head. "Nothing about this is your fault."

"She was mad at me. Hazel hates me," I said. "That's why Arthur died."

He pulled me closer. "No, love. She hates me. She resents me for moving to America, for falling in love with you. Hazel took her anger at me out on your family, and I'm sorry for that."

I closed my eyes and squeezed tighter against his rock-hard chest. I felt the marble of his body against my own firm form. His skin was cold — the same as mine.

"I'm sorry about the wedding," he whispered. "You deserved better than that."

"It doesn't matter," I mumbled. "I'm still your wife. We have bigger problems, though. My sister's boyfriend is dead. I don't even know what to do."

"I know, little dove, I know," he mumbled against my hair.

We sat silently for a few moments. The only sound was Penny sucking her bottle. I could hear her little heart pounding in her chest. She was so strong, yet so small. I would protect her as long as I lived. Even if it meant I had to deal with Hazel for the rest of my life, I would never stop fighting for her.

"What did you do with Hazel?" I asked.

"I locked her in a cell in the basement," he replied.

I looked up. "You have holding cells in the basement?"

He nodded. "James wasn't the first vampire in Savannah to go on a murder spree. I originally tried to reason with them, to bring back their humanity, but it rarely ever worked. It was a vampire rehab of sorts. But when we tried letting them back into the world, they went back to killing humans. It didn't work. Vampirism isn't for everyone. Some people simply can't handle it. They have addictive personalities."

I bit my lip. The memory of James' face when I had killed him came to mind. His eyes had pleaded with me. Even though he had lost his memories to some sort of supernatural amnesia, a part of his soul recognized me. I had loved him so much. After so many years of being alone, James's love made me realize I could live again. He had brought happiness into my life. James was never meant to be my forever, but he was one of my epic loves. I could never forget him or rid myself of the memory of his smile. Still, he was never really meant to be mine. Not every beautiful love was intended to last. I wasn't sure if that made it less special or not. James had brought out the light in my life, and I would always remember him for that. James had given me hope.

Vampirism had been the worst thing to ever happen to him. Looking back, I should have let him die. When he had been kidnapped and tortured by a sadistic werewolf, I decided that changing him was my only option. But his injuries had caused him to lose his memories—his sense of morality. I wondered if Hazel had been the same way. She hadn't lost her memories, but vampirism wasn't good for her. She couldn't control herself. But she was Albert's sister, and he didn't want to kill her. Could we just keep her locked in the basement forever? No, that wasn't right. We couldn't keep her in a cell for the next few centuries. And to be honest, I didn't think Hazel would change, no matter how much time she had to reconsider murderous ways. I didn't want to be in the same building as her. What would Anya think?

"I haven't decided what to do with her yet," he said.

I laced my fingers behind his neck, wondering how I was supposed to handle the knowledge that my murderous, lunatic sister-in-law was in my basement.

Chapter Five
WHEN THE STARS COME OUT

It was around three in the morning, and the penthouse was dark. The only illumination came from a few candles on the side of the living room and the light of the moon. It was almost entirely silent. It was as if all motion in the world had stopped. There was simply darkness and an overwhelming lack of sound. No music, no breeze, nothing.

Penny was asleep in her nursery. She slept well for a baby. We were vampire parents who didn't sleep, yet she was perfectly content to rest all night. Albert was sitting in the nursery watching her. Sometimes he would stay there for hours. He watched the way she breathed and wondered what her dreams were about. For a moment, I stood and admired them.

As I wandered back to our bedroom, I caught a glimpse of something out of the corner of my eye. It was dark but almost nonexistent, like the shadow of emptiness. I turned with vampire speed, but nothing was there. I shook my head in frustration; it was probably just stress. Then it happened again. The movement was fast and sharp. I spun but saw nothing. The darkness of the room was untouched. I could hear no heartbeat or indication of a person, living or dead. There were a few moments of stunning, frozen air. I felt no movement whatsoever. My marble form was as stiff as stone.

But then — in a soft, desperate voice — I heard my name, yet I saw no form. My head seemed to be spinning. I turned all around the room, but there was no one there. Again, the room became quiet. Before I had a chance to think, whispers started erupting all around me. It was as if a million little voices were hissing in my ears. I tried to ignore them, but they seemed to echo. They weren't coming from a singular place but all around. I squeezed my eyes shut and placed my hands over my ears. Still, the voices grew louder. No matter how hard I tried to block them out, they pounded into my brain. Yelling, crying, and whispers of anger flew around the room, pushing further and further into my mind.

When I opened my eyes, I gasped. It seemed as if everything was frozen. Time stood still as I tried to process the sight before me. James was standing there. It was impossible; I had witnessed his body turn to ash. He couldn't be alive. It was literally impossible — vampires couldn't come back from the dead. I didn't know what to do. After all, it couldn't be real. How was I supposed to react? James stood before me with tattered, bloody clothes and a dagger in his chest. His face was pale and death-like.

"James," I whispered.

He frowned. "This is your fault."

I gasped. My heart seemed to break into shards all over again. I had thought it was already in a million pieces, but hearing those words come out of his mouth made me want to collapse in pain. There was a piece of myself that believed him. After all, he had only become a vampire because of me. If I had never entered his life, he would be a healthy college student.

"I'm dead. I never would have died if I hadn't met you," he said in a calm, poisonous voice.

My head was pounding. It was as if my brain was pulsing within my skull. I could barely focus on anything other than the nausea that flooded my body. I began to shake, unable to hold my body still.

"I'm sorry, James," I pleaded.

"You can't bring me back, Anne. You have to live with this forever. You have blood on your hands." James scowled at me.

I bit my lip. A choked sob escaped my mouth. My insides were churning. It was my fault, all of it. He was right; I had killed him. He should have still been a human teenager. James could have gone to college and been anything he wanted to be. He could have been a doctor; he would have been good at that. But now, he would never have the chance to do those things.

Why had I fallen in love with him? It had to be those gorgeous green eyes. I remembered the way his hands had fluttered over my hips. My skin grew cold at the thought. His lips had been so soft, like rose petals. I should have known better. He deserved more than death.

"I didn't mean for it to happen, James," I whispered in a shattered voice.

He shook his head. "But it did."

And moments later, he was gone. The room was back to normal, and there were no more whispering voices. The night was quiet. I could hear a soft breeze out the window, but that was all. My head was no longer pounding, but there was an ache in my chest.

I jumped as the bedroom door opened. Albert entered the room. His hair was all jumbled, and his eyes were dark. His dress shirt was unbuttoned, and I could see the beginning of his hard, muscled abdomen. There was the familiar warm sensation in the front of my stomach. Everything was tight. I felt as if I had fallen from a cool waterfall and ended up in a steamy river. My whole body was a mess of confusing emotions. I felt everything from sorrow to passion. Albert smiled a full, heart-stopping grin. "Mrs. Jefferson."

"Hi," I stuttered.

He slipped his shoes off and walked toward me. When

he reached me, he placed his hands on my hips, gently rubbing his finger against the fabric of my dress. Strangely, they were extremely tender. He dotted fluttering kisses upon my neck, creating a trail of soft caresses. I wrapped my arms around him and held his body as if he was my anchor to sanity.

I was allured by the way his pants conformed to his sculpted legs, the way his shirt hung open, exposing his muscular chest, and the contour of his neck. Everything about Albert captured my heart. Even the most mundane things about him caused a flutter in my stomach. His biceps were strong and defined, leading my eyes to drift all over his body. Albert's chiseled form looked as if he belonged in a magazine. He had the appearance of a fairytale hero. Except, he definitely wasn't the knight in shining armor. Albert was the dark, mysterious king that occupied European legends. I would never become bored looking at him. His very presence made my body feel alive and jelly-like all at once. I could hardly form coherent thoughts.

"It's late, little dove," he mumbled against me.

"I know," I replied.

Albert gently lifted me up so that my head was against his shoulder. I buried my face against him and closed my eyes. I wanted to forget whatever had just happened. Albert was my safe place. He could make it all better. My fingers gripped his silken locks. He slowly brushed my hair away and planted his lips in the center of my neck.

He was my Heathcliff, my protector, my–husband. It would take time to get used to. I could hardly picture him as anything other than the mysterious man I had always thought him to be. But now, he would always be mine.

"Is it alright if I...," he stopped as if waiting for an answer.

"Yes," I whispered.

And less than a single moment later, his fangs sunk into my neck.

Chapter Six
SOMEONE TO BLAME

The memorial was taking place at a small venue tucked away near the beach. Anya had moved out of the apartment complex. She couldn't handle being in the place where Arthur had died, and I certainly understood that. I hadn't talked to her since the wedding, and seeing her again made me extremely anxious. Nina and Anya were both staying in a hotel, and Arthur had enlisted a vampire psychologist to check on them. I hadn't even known there was such a person. But, of course, Albert had been able to find one. Nina was watching Anya like a hawk. I'd never heard of a vampire committing suicide before, but the psychologist was worried. Roy was staying with them, too. He had barely spoken to anyone. His sister was already dead, and now his brother was gone. Roy and Arthur had expected to have forever as vampires. For a few moments, eternity had seemed endless, but forever hadn't lasted very long.

Albert had been watching me strangely, too. I hadn't told him about the...incident. I wasn't sure if seeing James had been a hallucination, but it certainly felt real. He had shaken all my perceptions about his death. All of my insecurities had flooded to the front of my mind. Yes, my guilt had been there before. But after I saw James, it was so much more evident. Whether or not I had really spoken to James—or I was just going crazy—I felt like a monster. Being with Albert had made me feel more okay with being a vampire. I had managed to take care of our daughter for months now. She was alive and well. I hadn't even known it was possible for a vampire to do such a thing. But this was all getting to me, and I wasn't sure what to do.

It seemed as if all the tragedies that befell my family could be blamed on me. James had died because I turned him into a vampire without considering how he would handle the transition. Roy and Arthur's sister had only become a vampire because of James—which, in a roundabout way, was my doing, too. And now Arthur was dead because of Albert's lunatic sister, who was only in Savannah because of our wedding. It all came down to me. Maybe it would have been better if I had just stayed the lonely vampire girl pining after her ex-boyfriend, who would have been in his nineties if he were still alive.

We were all shrouded in black. I wore a long, velvet evening gown and high stiletto heels. My hair was pulled into a sleek ponytail at the base of my neck, and my gorgeous new wedding ring was displayed on my finger. There was no color on my face other than the deep red of my lips. I truly felt like a vampire, but not in a good way.

Albert — wearing one of his classic black suits — carried Penny in his arms. She was, of course, completely unaware of much of what was going on. Other than Nina, Roy, and Anya, we were the only vampires in the room.

The place was filled with werewolves. Before transitioning, Arthur had been the alpha of his pack. They were huddled around Roy, watching us with suspicion. The air was filled with anxious energy. They blamed us for everything that had happened to Arthur. People could turn on each other so quickly. We were all supernatural, but when the pain struck, it was easy to find someone to blame. Vampires turned on werewolves, and werewolves turned on vampires. We were only a little ways away from a conflict. Not today, though. We all valued Arthur's memory too much. Besides, Roy had once been a werewolf, too. He would be loyal to Nina, and the wolves wouldn't want to move against him.

The wolves looked at us with hate-filled eyes, though. I had never seen such fury directed at me — except perhaps from Hazel. This was new and extremely uncomfortable. Never in my life had I actually tried to offend someone. In fact, I had isolated myself in order to avoid conflict. As a human girl, things had been so simple. We had been the heroes, and the Nazis had been the villains. I remembered the war. America had been so united, everyone joining together as friends. My childhood had been filled with handsome men in army uniforms, women taking care of our homeland, and an overall sense of understanding that we were truly all in the war together. The modern world wasn't the same.

But as a vampire, everything was different. Why had things changed so much? I didn't even remember it happening. It was kind of like watching yourself grow up; you didn't realize it had occurred until you were a young adult. On occasion, I looked in the mirror and forgot I was a vampire. Some days...I felt as if I was playing pretend. But when the werewolves looked at me with menace, I remembered. It was impossible to forget your identity when someone hated you for it. It was like a storybook, not a Disney fairytale, but rather a Brothers Grimm nightmare. I was the monster, and their looks made my perceived identity rather clear. Not all hate had to be communicated verbally or physically — sometimes, one glance was enough.

"I don't know how long I can stay here," I whispered.

"Through the dedication?" Albert asked.

Penny began to fuss, and he handed her to me. I held her so that her head was against my shoulder. She immediately fell asleep, totally unaware that her mother was a vampire. That in itself amazed me; she truly didn't know the difference. I wasn't sure of the definitions of good and evil, but I did know that Penny was the most innocent creature I had ever seen.

I nodded. "Okay."

He led me over to a few of the padded chairs, where we sat and waited. Eventually, members of Arthur's family began to speak. They told stories and laughed. For a while, Roy went up to talk about their early teen years. Anya went up for a few moments, but she became overwhelmed with pain before saying even a couple of words. Nina took Anya away to clear the running mascara from her face. Part of me wanted to go with them, but I decided not to. Albert and I sat silently. There wasn't anything we could say. We didn't even have a body to mourn over–that might have been the worst part. There was nothing but a collection of pictures and flowers to occupy the empty space. It was a pretty room with lush cream carpet and tasteful, caramel-colored walls. A shining chandelier hung from the ceiling, and candles scattered around the room. With the multitude of comfortable couches and padded chairs, everyone could remain physically comfortable. Yet it did seem hollow — very hollow. It was almost painfully empty.

I hated funerals. In that moment, I resolved to never attend one again if I could help it. I didn't want to be blamed for anyone else's death. Such accusations caused nausea to invade my body and uneasiness within my mind. I felt heavy guilt, but I wasn't sure what to do about it. After all, I couldn't go back to alter the past. All I could manage was an overwhelming self-hate.

After everyone finished speaking, the wolves dispersed to attend a remembrance dinner. Clearly, the vampires weren't invited. Albert and I quickly made our exit. Nina and Anya would come back later. Right now, Roy was doing all he could to remain calm. I was fairly sure he was still in shock. After all, his brother had died in front of him. We had all become so accustomed to trauma that we hardly recognized it anymore.

"I think it's time to go," Albert said.

Penny was still in my arms. She was fast asleep. I nodded, handing her to Albert before heading to the door. When we reached our car, he strapped Penny in the back before helping me inside. I was in a daze and unable to snap out of it. It seemed as if the world was spinning around me. I momentarily wondered if immortality was really worth all it entailed.

Chapter Seven
CHOICES

The dawn had just started breaking. The city was covered in fog, almost like London but hotter. The plants were exploding after the heavy rain. Vibrancy was everywhere except in my heart. Anya still hadn't spoken to me since the wedding. Nina had sent a few hurried text messages, but she was busy caring for Anya and Roy. I had offered to help, but Nina assured me she was fine. Albert was consumed with work. There was some sort of problem going on with one of his recently-opened businesses. He dabbled in just about every field. This was a restaurant in the Egyptian city of Alexandria. Albert had tried explaining why it was a good business opportunity, but I hadn't really understood. He promised to take me there sometime. But really, I could hardly focus on anything.

So Penny and I were alone most of the time. I had fallen into the daily monotony of taking care of my baby. All of the things I had previously enjoyed seemed dull. I felt like a horrible mother, a terrible sister, and a boring wife. I wasn't interested in Albert's business ventures. My family didn't want to see me, and I didn't take any enjoyment from caring for my daughter. There had to be a serious problem with me.

I could hear the buzzing again. The very sounds brought terror to my heart. It seemed to be following me around. This strange vibration in the air was almost strong enough to be tangible. Whenever I tried to think, it was like a dark cloud covering my mind. Everything seemed cold. The buzzing was getting louder. It was all I could hear and one of the most painful physical sensations I had ever experienced. The room seemed to spin as I tried to see clearly. When I closed my eyes, just like before, everything got louder.

"Anne," James said.

With fear, I turned around to find him before me. He was in the same bedraggled state as when he had died. Our eyes were locked together in a fierce, untrusting embrace. Suddenly, I felt unsafe. It was as if he was holding a metaphorical stake to my heart. I was freezing, and there was no airflow. Everything was frigid, his stare included. It was as if we were the only people left in the world, and that thought was petrifying. I was shaking, and my breathing was staggered. Seeing him like that, with blood covering his torn clothes, felt like being stabbed in a hundred different ways. There was shock, nausea, and guilt, all wrapped into a blanket of pain. I didn't want to talk to him or hear his name again.

I wanted to forget the way I had loved him and move on in peace.

"Have you ever thought about dying?" James asked.

I took a step back. "What?"

"Dying," he said, "I know you've wondered about it. There must have been times you wished you could grow old. I know you, Anne. You didn't want immortality. You don't deserve it, either."

"What are you talking about?" I whispered.

He pursed his lips. "Please, you know you've felt it. There's some part of you that longs for an escape. Don't you want to be able to close your eyes and fade away into unconsciousness? You wouldn't have to live with the guilt."

"Dying isn't my goal," I replied.

"But is it your desire?" James said in a clipped tone.

I simply stared at him. How could I respond to the hallucination of my ex-boyfriend? Then again, maybe it wasn't a hallucination. What if it was real? Had he somehow come back from the dead? No, his body had turned to ash. But why did I keep seeing him? I wasn't dwelling on James. In fact, I wasn't doing much thinking at all. I was trying to simply take care of Penny and be as attentive to Albert as possible. Albert had been showering me with all sorts of gifts. Maybe it was his way of making up for our delayed honeymoon. He brought me a fresh bouquet of flowers every day. Our penthouse was practically filled with the sweet aroma of floral scents. While he was away at meetings or dealing with matters outside the apartment, he often sent romantic, handwritten letters or notes of endearment. It brightened my spirits but couldn't lift this overwhelming darkness.

"I don't know who you are, but you're not James," I said.

"Of course I am," he replied. "I'm your perception of him. I'm the visible representation of your inner thoughts about the man you used to love. You might not realize it, but you can't stop thinking about me. The guilt is overwhelming you. There's no hiding the truth. You don't deserve to be alive."

"You're wrong," I said in a determined tone.

"Am I?" James asked. "I can only say what you think. After all, I'm only a visible representation of your thoughts."

"I don't think about those things," I said.

"You can tell yourself that," he retorted.

"Go away!" I shouted.

He shrugged. "You know I'll be back."

Moments later, he faded away. I collapsed on the ground in pain, confusion, and fear. Every inch of me was shaking. I didn't have enough strength to hold myself up. The whole world seemed to be vibrating. My head fell to the ground. Vampires weren't supposed to feel weak. That wasn't how supernatural strength worked. Every piece of literature I had ever read told me I was supposed to be practically unstoppable with overwhelming stamina and superhuman confidence. But at that moment, I didn't feel powerful. In fact, I felt incredibly weak. It was as if my whole body was barely able to move. I felt like time was dragging behind me as I struggled to hold myself together. Every cell in my body was fighting my efforts to remain calm.

Penny began crying and snapped me out of my daze. Immediately, I seemed to regain my strength. I stood from the floor and made my way over to her bassinet. Picking her up, I noticed her bottle was empty. Then, I began to walk toward the kitchen. I moved without thought or control. After pouring her a fresh bottle of milk, I sat down and placed her on my lap. She leaned back against me as she gently sucked on her bottle.

I tried to clear my mind, but I couldn't. It was all just too real. Even if this James was a figment of my imagination, his words were true. I did deserve to die. After all, several of the people I loved had died because of me. That was enough, wasn't it? I had signed my own death warrant. If Hazel didn't end up escaping and killing me, the guilt would. I didn't even trust myself. What would I do in a moment of weakness? What could James persuade me to do? I didn't feel sane. In fact, it seemed as if I was losing my mind. It was like a strange force was inhabiting my body, and my mind had taken a backseat.

"Hey baby, I'm back," Albert said as he walked through the door.

His voice brought relief to my terror-filled heart. I felt a little bit safer. My body visibly relaxed in his presence. For a moment, I could forget about whatever had just happened. Albert was like a cool summer rain rinsing away the overwhelming heat of a suffocating desert. His presence was an oasis filled with the only oxygen I could find.

I snapped out of my inner contemplation. "How was work?"

"The usual," he replied.

I watched as he took his suit jacket off and loosened his tie. A few moments of silence passed as I was unable to shake my anxiety. It felt as if a weight was pressing down upon my chest. There was something I desperately needed to know.

"What are you going to do with Hazel?" I asked.

He paused for a moment before sitting down beside me. There had been a time when Albert and his sister were inseparable. They had survived so much together, including their human deaths. But when Hazel had tried to kill Penny, their bond shattered. Albert didn't tolerate the unnecessary killing of humans, and he certainly wouldn't allow a child to be hurt. His humanity was one of my favorite things about him. But even though Hazel had tried to kill our daughter and caused the death of Arthur, he still felt affection for her. She was his sister. He could never stop loving her.

"I honestly don't know. She's still locked in a holding cell in the basement," he replied.

There was so much pain in his eyes. He looked torn between compassion and duty. I could practically feel his stress. So much of this had become his responsibility.

"So you're going to keep her alive?" I asked.

He looked down. "I can't kill her, Anne. I just can't do it."

I sat staring out the window. There was nothing to say. Would my mind be pacified if Hazel was dead? Was that the only way to make my subconscious version of James go away?

"I'm sorry, Anne," he whispered.

I wrapped my arms around him and pulled his head to mine. I focused on his breathing, trying to calm my mind. He was only trying to take care of everyone. I couldn't fault him for loving too much. Everyone had at least one project-type person in their life, and Hazel was his.

I ran my hand down his back. "Do what you have to do."

"I think you should see a psychologist," he replied.

I pursued my lips. "Why?"

He looked into my eyes. "You've experienced a lot of trauma lately. Not to mention the nature in which you were turned. You have a lot of pain inside you, which is unhealthy. I know you won't talk to me about it. That's alright, I understand. But you need to talk to someone, even if you won't admit it."

I shook my head. "I don't want to see anyone."

He stood and crossed his arms. "It's not a request, Anne."

I slumped back against the couch and turned away from him. Penny was still cuddled up in my arms. She seemed blissfully unaware of the nature of our discussion. I pulled her to my chest. She was the most real thing I could feel.

Albert sighed before shaking his head. "The psychologist will be here tomorrow."

I looked up at him with wide eyes. "Please, I don't want to talk to anyone."

Albert's eyes seemed to hold fire. "You will, whether you want to or not."

With nothing else to say, he walked away.

Chapter Eight
HOW DO YOU FEEL?

"Mrs. Jefferson, your husband has informed me of your past. What would you like to discuss first?" Niko asked.

He was a tall, dark-skinned vampire with wide eyes and a head full of handsome hair. Niko was dressed impeccably in a gray suit, white dress shirt and black tie. Niko appeared completely relaxed as he looked at me with patience and a kind smile. Having him in my living room felt strange, considering we rarely allowed strangers into the penthouse.

"There's nothing I want to talk about," I replied.

He nodded. "Let's start at the beginning and work our way up then."

He was very determined to get answers out of me. I wasn't sure if it was Albert's influence, but Niko was extremely persistent. His determination was stronger than a wall of stone.

I sighed. "Alright."

Niko smiled. "So, at seventeen, you were violently murdered, assaulted, and turned into a vampire. Is that correct?"

That event was on my list of top five things I didn't want to talk about. But he was going to address the issue whether I wanted him to or not, so remaining silent wouldn't do much good.

I bit my lip. "Yes."

"And how does that make you feel?" Niko asked.

No, he wouldn't understand. The violation I had felt that horrible night was beyond description. It was too intense, too raw to communicate. I couldn't tell him how I felt because he simply wouldn't be able to process it. Besides, I actively avoided thinking about the event.

I looked into his eyes. "I've never really stopped to think about it."

He raised his eyebrows. "Well, now is the perfect opportunity."

He wouldn't let it go. I had to give it to him. Niko was a very charming individual. He could probably convince most people to talk, but not me. This was not something I wanted to address.

I shook my head. "I really don't want to. I don't think you understand how hard I've worked to get past it."

He nodded. "Mrs. Jefferson, there is no way to process your trauma without acknowledging it."

Well, I could try. If it would help the hallucination go away, I would attempt it. He wouldn't be able to fully understand, but I would try. I had never opened up to someone like this, not Nina, Anya, James, or Albert. But what I had to say wasn't pretty.

There weren't any words to really explain how that night affected my life. Of course, I had died that night. But it had done more to my mind than my body. Ever since becoming a vampire, I'd been plagued by low self-esteem and the inability to love myself.

I looked at the floor. "I felt dirty, almost as if my whole body had been ruined. It seemed as if I was damned, like I was in my own personal hell."

His eyes immediately filled with sympathy. I didn't want that. The idea of being pitied made me feel nauseous. It had been a lifetime ago and wasn't worth dwelling on. I just wanted to forget it.

"I see," he murmured. "I understand that your former boyfriend, Gale, was also killed on the night you became a vampire."

No, not this. I didn't want to talk about Gale. He didn't belong in this conversation. I wanted my memory of him to be clouded by how long ago he had died. He deserved to have his memory preserved in a peaceful way.

"Yes," I whispered.

"Do you talk about him, Anne?" Niko asked.

I shook my head. Clearly, I didn't. It wasn't hard to tell how uncomfortable I was. My insides felt like they were being twisted and pulled in all the wrong directions. It was as if a hurricane was raging in my chest.

He looked down at his notepad. "And why not?"

He wouldn't understand this, either. There was no way to truly understand the horrible knowledge that you had survived when you should have been dead. It was as if I was a flower that had survived a harsh winter when I should have withered away. It felt unnatural, like a freakish mistake.

"Guilt," I whispered.

He took a moment to write a few things down. I bit my lip again; it was becoming a habit. I wanted to close my eyes and float away. For just one moment, I wished I could disappear.

"Anne, you have nothing to feel guilty about. You are not the villain in this story. This is a classic case of survivor's guilt," he replied.

"I don't know why you're so sure," I whispered.

He placed his notepad down beside him. "You were an innocent seventeen-year-old girl in the 1950s wishing for a calm, domestic life. By no fault of your own, you happened to catch the eye of a sadistic vampire with desires we will not discuss during this particular meeting. He murdered your boyfriend and changed you into a vampire. You have absolutely no fault in this. You were an innocent victim."

"But if it weren't for me, Gale wouldn't be dead," I replied.

He shook his head. "Anne, if it weren't for you, Penny wouldn't be alive."

I leaned back in my chair. Crossing my arms over my chest, I looked at the floor. My stilettos were digging into the carpet. Suddenly, my little black dress felt a bit too tight. The amount of heat in the room was suffocating.

Niko sighed. "After becoming a vampire, you met your sisters, Nina and Anya. You lived with them for years while isolating yourself and not participating in any romantic relationships. After many years alone, you met James Hamilton and started a relationship with him. Then, you were forced to let James die as a human or change him into a vampire. Is that correct?"

I nodded. "Yes, but it was my fault he was hurt in the first place. If I hadn't entered into a relationship with him—"

Niko held up his hand. "Mrs. Jefferson, the more you try to convince me of your guilt, the more it will implant the thoughts within your own mind. You are simply making this harder on yourself."

I slumped back in my chair. The room seemed to chill. I could almost feel the silence. My skin was prickly, and my legs were unstable.

Niko raised his eyebrows. "Never before have I had a client try to paint themselves as a villain. You are clearly an empath with a serious self-esteem problem and chronic depression. Combined with your survivor's guilt, that puts you in a very low, lonely place."

My mouth dropped open. "Excuse me?"

He smiled. "Mrs. Jefferson, vampire therapy is quite different from a human's. I am one of the few supernatural therapists in the world, and my methods differ from many other mental health professionals' practices. I am blunt and honest."

"How do you know so much about me?" I asked.

He pulled a stack of papers out of his bag. "This is the detailed account your husband gave me."

I scowled at the stack. Of course, Albert was always a few steps ahead of me. I didn't even want to read what he had written. There were at least five hundred pages in the stack. No doubt I wouldn't like it.

Niko picked up his notepad. "Back to James. It is my understanding that you were the one to end his immortal life. Is that correct?"

I nodded. "Yes."

He jotted something down. "Do you realize that by ending his life, you saved countless humans? He was going on a killing spree, and he would have murdered many more if you hadn't stopped him."

I bit my lip. "We could have imprisoned him instead."

He sighed. "You need to ask yourself if that would

have provided justice for his victims. And even if it would have, how long would you have been able to keep him contained? Forever is a very long time, Anne. I have lived for over five hundred years, and in my experience, vampires with uncontrollable blood lust cannot be reformed. There are...anomalies, but they are incredibly rare."

All I could see was James's bright green eyes. I was so dizzy, and the room started to spin. I wanted to throw up. It felt as if I was spinning at the speed of light. My head was clouded with confusion and pain. The whispers were floating up around me again, and I could feel their presence. The voices were haunting, like that of an evil spirit. It was a terrifying nightmare, the kind where you could only sense darkness and agony. James would be back. He would torment me again. But...did I deserve it?

"Mrs. Jefferson, are you alright?" Niko asked.

I felt as if a hammer was pounding inside my head. My whole body seemed to shake. I could barely breathe because my lungs felt as if they were collapsing. If I had been standing, I would have fallen over. My nails were pressing into the fabric of the chair. Niko was saying something, but I couldn't hear him.

The whispers kept getting louder. They were angry and resentful. Who were these voices? I didn't know. Perhaps they were James's victims. Did they blame me for all of it? Was I their real murderer? That was a philosophical question that I probably couldn't answer. Maybe there wasn't even one true response, but that didn't change the way my chest contracted with pain.

And there he was—James stood in front of me with a stake in his hand. All I could do was scream because I couldn't even manage to move. There was fear in every inch of my body. It was primal, like that of an animal in the wild. My vocal cords were on fire, but I couldn't even hear the screams of terror escaping my mouth—I could only feel them. I felt unable to do anything about it. That was the worst part— being so terrified that I couldn't even move. I truly thought I was going to die, and I wasn't sure of my opinion on the matter. All I knew was that my heart was filled with terror, and the world stood still.

I watched—frozen—as James lunged toward me and shoved the dagger into my heart. And all of a sudden, everything was gone.

Chapter Nine
HIDDEN ENEMY

Albert was shaking me. There was no dagger, and my body was completely intact. When I saw him, I stopped screaming. The room was silent.

"Anne! What happened?" Albert asked.

I looked from him to the therapist. Niko sat in his hair with a look of shock on his face. I didn't know what to tell them; they would never believe me. It was all crazy. I didn't want them to think I had lost my mind. Then again, had I?

"I—I don't know," I whispered.

Albert scooped me up into his arms. "You need to rest."

I didn't reply. Niko waited in the living room as Albert carried me into the bedroom and closed the door behind us. He lay me down on the bed and removed my shoes. After wrapping a blanket around me, he sat on the corner of the bed. Albert was eyeing me warily. I could tell he was scared, not for himself, but for me. There were a few moments where we just stared at each other. Neither of us knew what to say. I didn't know how to make him feel better. He didn't need to know the full extent of things. After all, he wasn't at fault. I didn't want him to be plagued by my hallucinations.

"Anne, I want you to wait here," he said as if talking to a child.

There wasn't any doubt that I would stay where I was; I was still too terrified to move. I simply nodded and watched as he carefully stood and walked to the door. With one last glance at me, he walked out of the room. I wanted him to stay with me, but he needed to talk to Niko. Honestly, I didn't know how much good it would do. Neither of them understood what was happening. All they could do was speculate, and I certainly wasn't going to reveal the truth.

Albert and Niko tried to talk softly, but I could hear them. I knew they probably thought I couldn't. Yet I was listening as closely as I could, and I managed to hear every word.

"What is wrong with her? Did you do something?" Albert hissed.

There was a pause before Niko spoke. "I believe she's suffering from psychosis as a result of survivor's guilt and depression. Clearly, she had a hallucination. Now, I don't know if it was her first, but it probably won't be her last."

"What? She's a vampire; that makes no sense. We are supernatural beings with incredible power. Her mind isn't that weak," he replied.

Niko's voice was calm. "There's a first for everything. Her mind is fractured, and it has been for a very long time."

Albert's whisper was almost scary. "Fix her."

"I can't," Niko replied. "There are some treatments— some therapies, but no cure. I can only do what I've been doing. Human medicine would have no effect on her. This is the most complex case I have ever worked with."

I heard the shattering of glass. "That's not acceptable!" Albert roared.

"I'm sorry, Mr. Jefferson," Niko said with patience. "I would be more than happy to work with the two of you if you think your presence would help stabilize her. After all, we don't know how many hallucinations she's had. There's never been one in front of you, though. Perhaps you drive them off. I have no science or studies to go on. This is completely new."

Albert regained some composure. "She won't talk with me in the room, not about anything important."

I suddenly felt very guilty. Did he think I was keeping things from him? The only secrets I had kept had been to prevent him from thinking I was crazy. But now that he knew I was hallucinating, what would he do? Albert might stop loving me. Why would he want a wife with a fractured mind? I had gone crazy, and he had no idea how to make my hallucinations go away.

"Mr. Jefferson, she is not safe by herself. You can't

leave her alone," Niko whispered.

"Why not?" Albert asked.

Niko paused. "I do not believe she is safe. She is a danger to herself. I don't think she would hurt you or your daughter, but I do think in a moment of mental instability, something very terrible could occur."

"Anne wouldn't do that," Albert retorted.

"She's not in her right mind. These aren't her actions. The depression has taken hold of her," Niko whispered.

Albert sighed. "Alright, but I expect intensive therapy. As many times a day as you need, I want you to fix her!"

Niko took a deep breath. "I will certainly try."

I heard the front door shut as Niko left the penthouse. Albert was left standing in the living room. Penny was with a babysitter. After a few moments, he came back into the bedroom. I hadn't moved from where he had placed me.

Albert smiled. "You're going to be alright. Don't worry."

I tried to smile back, but I couldn't after the conversation I had overheard. I felt frozen in place. My mind was swimming with possibilities. Were my thoughts even my own? Did I belong to myself anymore? I felt invaded. My body seemed like a shell and hardly worth protecting. My mind was working against me, and I had no idea what thoughts were safe and which ones were hazardous.

Albert lay down beside me and pulled me against his

chest. I felt his hard body beneath me as he shifted, so I was on top of him. We had held each other this way countless times before, but this felt more desperate. Wrapping my arms around his neck, I held on as if he was the only thing tethering me to the earth. Albert seemed to be the only road to sanity I had left. I squeezed him so hard I was afraid I would hurt him, but then he wrapped his arms around me with just as much strength, and I knew we were both terrified. I had never seen Albert so afraid. This was the man who had helped me become comfortable with being a vampire. He was so confident in who he was and had made me feel the same way. But now, I lay in his arms, afraid of what I might do if I let go.

I wanted to kiss him, but I was afraid that he might turn away. Would he want to kiss his crazy, unstable wife? Was I so far gone that he felt nothing for me? Maybe I was just his form of charity. I was hallucinating about my dead boyfriend and really believed he would kill me. Was there any sane part of me left?

I didn't feel safe, not in the least. I wasn't even sure if I could trust myself with Penny. What if I dropped her... or worse. My mind was a mess of panic and fear. Did I need to be locked in a cell right along with Hazel? Was I that far gone? Albert didn't seem to think so, but he was optimistic. The therapist had told him there was no medicine that would work. Would more of that uncomfortable therapy actually make a difference? I wasn't sure, but I didn't trust my judgment.

Chapter Ten
MY OWN UNIVERSE

"Anne?" Albert whispered.

I sat up and propped myself against the pillows on the bed. It had been two hours since my last hallucination. Albert looked more disheveled than I had ever seen him, and his eyes were shrouded in fear-stricken hesitancy. Seeing him so distressed made me feel sick. There was something purely wrong about Albert Jefferson being panicked. It was like a lion cowering in the presence of a lamb.

"Yes?" I whispered back.

He walked over to sit on the other side of the bed. There were moments of absolute silence while we just looked at each other. This was becoming a habit because we didn't know what else to do. His eyes ended up landing on my chest…right over my heart.

Albert attempted to put a note of optimism in his voice. "I think a change of scenery would be best."

I looked into his worry-filled eyes. "Are you sure that's safe? I mean, to let me be in front of humans. I'm not sure what I might do."

I didn't want to hallucinate in front of a crowd of people. It would draw attention to us, which was always bad for vampires. Blending in, or staying hidden, was the only way to go unnoticed.

He took my hands in his. "It's just going to be the two of us."

I felt a sudden ping of hesitancy. "What about Penny?"

"She's going to stay with a babysitter. I promise she'll be perfectly fine. We'll only be away for a week, just long enough to get some air," he replied.

I nodded, briefly wondering if perhaps a babysitter was safer for her than me right now. I didn't want to risk hurting Penny. Neither of us would ever recover from that, and I would never be able to stop hating myself.

"Where are we going?" I asked.

His face lit up with excitement. "Scotland."

A few months ago, I had briefly mentioned wanting to go to Scotland. Apparently, Albert had taken the request seriously. Well, it would at least be distracting. I had never been there, but it had always been a dream destination.

Albert gave me a very satisfied grin. "And we don't even have to worry about reservations or humans getting in our way because I've already bought a cottage. Here, let me show you."

He pulled a picture out of his pocket and handed it to me. It was a tiny white-brick house with a brown roof and chimney. It was charming and warm, almost like a fictional scene. Surrounding the house were lots of waist-high shrubs with tiny purple flowers. Leading up to the front door was a stone walkway adjourned by two wooden posts and hanging lanterns. Surrounding the cottage was nothing but green hills and a bright blue sky shrouded by a thick mist. Albert must have purchased the most fairytale-like house he could find.

"When did you buy this?" I asked.

He smiled confidently. "Right before the wedding. It was going to be a present for you, but I forgot about it."

I was tempted to laugh. Only Albert could forget about purchasing a house. Something like that probably wouldn't have slipped my mind. Then again, this was the third residence we owned…that I knew about.

"Thank you," I whispered.

Reaching over to the nightstand, I pulled open the door and retrieved a little black box. It was tied with a white ribbon and no bigger than the palm of my hand. I placed it on the bed between us.

He gave me a curious glance. I smiled back, and he picked it up. I watched as he carefully removed the ribbon and gently opened the clasp.

"I forgot about your present, too," I said.

His eyes grew wide as he lifted the chain out and clicked open the little golden compartment. The Tower of London was engraved on the front. Once his eyes landed on the picture inside, a look of warmth passed over him.

"It's us," I whispered, "when we were in London for the first time."

He closed it and lifted the chain to hang it around his neck. It hung directly over his heart, just where I had intended. He held it for a minute before looking back at me.

Albert leaned over and placed a soft kiss on my lips. I leaned into him, relishing in the taste of his lips and inhaling the sweet scent of mint. I wasn't going to pull away, but he did.

"Thank you," he mumbled against my lips. "Let's pack our things. We can rest on the plane.

~*~

After giving Penny a quick kiss on the cheek and ensuring she was in the hands of a highly-qualified babysitter, Albert and I boarded the plane. As soon as we entered, I stowed my suitcase in the luggage area and returned to the bedroom.

I wasn't surprised to find that it had been renovated. The once completely black apartment was now shrouded in shades of gray and soft pink. I had liked the black bedspread, but maybe Albert had found it too depressing. A few candles were lit beside the bed, and a diffuser released lavender oil. Albert seriously was trying to make me completely stress-free. At least he was succeeding in distracting me.

I slipped my white heels off and examined the small package on my side of the bed. It was a pink box with a large bow that I couldn't resist opening. Albert stood back to watch with a satisfied smile.

When I lifted the lid, it immediately fell to the floor. Inside the box were three first-print editions of *Emma*, *Little Women*, and *Shakespeare's Sonnets*. They were delicate books with slightly torn edges and bent spines. I ran my fingers across them, relishing in the feel of their well-worn covers.

"For me?" I asked.

Albert laughed softly. "Who else?"

I smiled up at him. "Thank you, they're wonderful."

He pulled me against him with my back to his front. Albert placed his hands on my hips and planted butterfly kisses on my neck. I leaned back and rested my head against his chest. Relaxing against him felt like sinking into a deep, comfortable sea of clouds. At his touch, the stress seemed to leave my body. I could feel his smile through the way his lips touched my skin.

"I thought you might like to add them to your collection," he whispered.

I turned to wrap my arms around his neck and nuzzle my head against his. Somehow, Albert made everything less overwhelming. He was so strong-willed that when I focused on him, nothing else could distract me. I loved the way he pulled my mind away from the things that scared me. It seemed too cliché, but Albert really was the anchor tethering me to the earth. He made me feel safe, more so than I ever had before. And I loved him with a passion stronger than anything else I had ever experienced. Even if I loved a hundred different men in multiple lifetimes, they could never compare to Albert. No matter how long my soul existed, he would forever be my heart's only desire.

"You are the most perfect thing I've ever seen," he mumbled against my ear, with his hands lost in the curls of my raven hair.

"And you are the only person keeping me alive," I whispered.

He pulled me harder against him and held me with a strength strong enough to contain the most skilled escape artist. If I had been human, I would have crumbled under his grasp. He knew just how hard he could hold me, though. Even though Albert was considerably stronger than me, he never hurt me.

"Oh, Anne, I love you too much to lose you," he said in the most desperate tone I had ever heard.

I could never leave him because it would break both of us. No matter how badly I wanted these hallucinations' pain and horror to disappear, Albert was always at the forefront of my mind. He was the only man I had ever loved with such ferocity, and my whole heart was devoted to him. Of course,

I loved Penny. But without Albert, I could never be a good mother. I wanted the best for her, and Albert was the key to that. He was my universe wrapped up into a man — a vampire. I gripped him harder. "I know. I love you too."

Chapter Eleven
FOREVER DEDICATED

Snow White's cottage was before me. It was small, cozy, and practically perfect. After landing in Scotland, we traveled over an hour to the outskirts of the highlands, where there was nothing but green surrounding us. The color was so vibrant that it made me unable to look away. In the distance were towering mountains with rubble from ancient castles that decorated the landscape. I wondered who had once lived there and when they had existed. Perhaps the former residents had been knights, riding around the mountains to save damsels in distress. The sky was clear and resembled the brightest of sapphires sparkling in the glimmer of the sun. It all seemed like a pleasant dream, like we had fallen into a storybook. The whole world felt so…alive. And in my experience, that was an uncommon thing.

I followed Albert through the sturdy wooden door and into the tiny living room. It was perhaps the most adorable place I had ever seen. The floor was a hard, cool stone that seemed to be consistent throughout the house. There was a giant fireplace with flowers sitting atop the mantle and blossoms falling down to frame the burning flames. On the far wall was a large leather couch and sturdy bookshelves on either side. There was a giant, brown, woven rug in the center of the room with a coffee table standing in the middle of it. The remaining walls were covered with built-in bookshelves stuffed to the brim with all sorts of literature. It all felt warm and cozy, the type of place where I could truly hide from the world. This was my own little oasis, a truly happy location. It was so secluded that I didn't even have to worry about being bothered by anyone else. We were safe in our little cottage.

Albert took my hand and led me through a small kitchen and back into the rest of the house. There was a bathroom with a large stone tub and matching shower. The room seemed like a paradise. Roses were placed on the vanity, and potted lavender plants were scattered throughout the room. It smelled like a flower garden. A large chandelier hung from the center of the ceiling where real wax candles burned to illuminate the little indoor paradise.

Further down the hall was Penny's room. I had no idea how Albert had arranged for the house to be renovated so quickly, but I decided not to ask. He had probably paid someone triple the usual cost to have it done in just a few days. Stepping into her room, I saw a wooden dollhouse accompanied by a stable, carriage, and tower. Beside it was a little crib with a large, plush baby doll dressed in a white gown with ribbons in her curly blonde hair. On the other side of the room was a large, stained-glass window depicting the ballroom scene from *Beauty and The Beast*. Beneath it was a short bookshelf that traveled the length of the wall. The top of the bookshelf was covered with a light pink cushion with small flowers embroidered on it. I laughed softly when I noticed that on the bottom row was a boxed collection of Harry Potter novels. A little bed covered with pink velvet pillows and a fluffy magenta comforter was on the only remaining wall. A large, stuffed unicorn with a sparkly horn and bright blue eyes rested on the bed. The room was perfect, so beautifully designed and personalized for our baby girl. I smiled at Albert, and he took my hand to lead me to the next room.

"I wasn't sure exactly how to arrange our bedroom, but I did my best," he said before opening the next door.

When I entered the room, my jaw dropped. Every single time Albert designed something for me, it was more impressive than the last. The stone floor was covered in a fluffy black carpet that spread the room's length. Hanging from the ceiling was an identical chandelier to the one in the bathroom, which illuminated the space in a soft, comforting light. Against one of the walls was a brown dresser with a vase of pink flowers sitting atop it. A large desk with stationery and a laptop was on the opposite side of the room. But the main piece of furniture in the space was a large, king-size bed with a dark wooden frame and a multi-colored quilt with pillows of the same pattern. It was all so…romantic.

Unlike our other bedrooms in London and Savannah, this room was not grand. It was comfortably small with a sweet, relaxed atmosphere that brought peace to my mind. I felt like I had been transported to a land of serenity where there was no crazy sister-in-law, hallucinations, or uncomfortable therapy sessions.

Albert slipped his boots off and sat down on the bed. "What do you think?"

My face lit up. "It's a beautiful room; I love it. But it doesn't even come close to the sight of my handsome husband sitting on our sweet country bed."

Love filled his eyes. "Come here, Anne."

I abandoned my cardigan on the dresser and crawled onto the bed beside him. His fingers landed in my hair and began to separate my curls. I felt his breath on my cheek as my body tingled from his close proximity.

"My sole purpose in this world is to take care of you and our daughter. Anything you need, it's yours," he whispered against my neck.

He placed kisses along my jaw, his lips fluttering against my skin. Every particle in my body felt alive. I loved his touch, scent, and feel–everything about him.

I nuzzled my head against his. "My only ever-present desire is to make you happy. I love you more than I know how to express. Because Albert, if I didn't have you, I don't think my soul would ever be complete. You are my strength. Being yours is my most satisfying occupation and my motivation to survive. I couldn't bear to abandon you because seeing the anguish in your eyes causes the greatest pain I have ever experienced."

I could feel his breath against my skin. His whispers somehow seemed more precious than diamonds. I treasured every single syllable that slipped from his lips. His words calmed the rush of emotions in my chest while making a new wave of happiness flow within my whole being. It was more than I could comprehend, yet not too much for my heart to understand.

He took my face in his hands. "I feel every sadness, joy, and loss that you do. Your pain is my pain, and your happiness is my happiness. Till death do us part, I am forever dedicated to maintaining your joy. It is my most important responsibility and will always be my greatest satisfaction."

"You save me every single day," I whispered.

His penetrating gaze examined my ocean eyes. "And you redeemed me, little dove."

I softly rested my head down beside his. He wrapped his arms around my waist and pulled me closer. Our lips touched and danced in the bliss only two people in all-consuming love could experience. In that moment, I lost myself in him.

Chapter Twelve
ALONE WITH YOU

"What is that for?" I asked.

Albert was holding up a large dress bag and smiling like a schoolboy. Nervousness began to flow through me. What could it possibly be? And what was it for? I wasn't sure I wanted to know, but I was going to find out.

"We are going to a party," he said with a huge smile.

Oh no, I thought, *not again*. I was beginning to seriously dislike parties. Besides, some of Albert's friends were — well — not the best company. I wasn't a huge fan of many of them.

I raised my eyebrows. "Do you remember the last time we went to a party? We have extremely bad luck with those."

He placed the bag beside me. "This one is being thrown by the largest coven in Scotland. The leader has requested we attend, and I didn't want to refuse. It'll be fun. Besides, it isn't nearly as formal as the last one we attended."

I unzipped the bag to find a knee-length, green plaid

Scottish dress. It was skin-tight but didn't expose anything. Along with it were a pair of fishnet tights and black stilettos. Behind the dress was a black blazer with tiny, green, embroidered vines on the front.

I raised my eyebrows. "Fishnet tights?"

Albert smirked. "Just an idea. You don't have to wear them."

I rolled my eyes. "Promise me you're not going to wear a kilt."

He laughed. "No, I'm wearing a suit."

"Good," I replied, "now leave me to change."

He gave me a satisfied smirk before leaving the bedroom and closing the door behind him. I pulled my suitcase open and retrieved my makeup bag. I wasn't going to wear anything other than eyeliner, mascara, and lipstick; vampires didn't have skin problems. I had no blemishes, dark circles, or pimples, only a pale, deathly-white face. Sometimes I wanted a little color, but I typically didn't mind my creamy skin. After quickly applying my small amount of makeup, I grabbed my hairbrush and piled my curls into a large bun on top of my head. It was loose and messy, but not in an unfashionable way. A few stray strands fell to frame my face and soften the style.

When I finished dressing, I left the room in search of Albert. He was standing in the bathroom, putting on his bow tie. I thought he didn't see me for a moment, but then his eyes met mine in the mirror. They widened with the unmistakable look of satisfaction and victory.

"Mrs. Jefferson," he whispered, "you look absolutely stunning."

I smiled and went to adjust his flawless yet untamable hair. "So do you."

He smirked. "Well, it's hard to compete with you."

I softly placed my hand against his cheek. "You only think that because you're so in love."

He placed a kiss on the back of my hand. "Then I intend to remain thoroughly entranced for as long as we both shall live."

I leaned up to give him a little kiss on the cheek before straightening his suit jacket. When I was satisfied, I took his hand and led him out the door. He let me lead him, and for the first time, I realized just how infatuated my husband really was.

When we arrived outside, I was met with the sight of a little carriage pulled by two black Shetland ponies. They were small horses with full coats and pretty, wide eyes. I grinned in excitement; I had always adored this breed. The driver, a middle-aged man — a vampire — tilted his hat in my direction. Albert smiled up at him. The carriage was the same dark color as the horses, with two padded seats and a small blanket.

The man stepped down. "Your horses, sir."

My jaw dropped; they were our horses? Albert would

never cease to surprise me. My eyes were glowing with thrill.

Albert nodded. "Anne, this is Joseph." Albert pointed back to a building I hadn't noticed before. It was a small barn, and I wondered how I hadn't seen it earlier. "That's the barn. Joseph and his wife, Becca, are the caretakers of the property. They live in the apartment above the barn."

I looked between them with a stunned expression. "These are our horses?"

Joseph nodded. "Yes, ma'am. Bonnie is on the right, and Cleo on the left."

Albert smiled. "I thought they would be a nice surprise for Penny. When she's older, we can bring her here so she can learn to ride."

I grinned. "Perfect."

Joseph stepped away from the carriage. "They're all yours."

Albert nodded. "Thank you."

He took my hand and lifted me up in the carriage. I sat with a silly grin, trying to conceal my excitement. The ponies were so cute, and I could barely believe they were actually ours. Penny would be so happy. Albert hopped up into the seat beside me and grabbed the reins. A moment later, we were off.

~*~

When we arrived at the party, the sun was setting. There were pink and orange clouds lighting up the sky with an array of colors. It was beautiful lighting, the kind that made everyone look more beautiful. A man came to take the reins from Albert and led our horses away to an area filled with cars and carriages. I looked around in awe at the outdoor setting. A large dance floor was set up with hanging lanterns and fairy lights all around. On the outskirts of the gathering, large bonfires illuminate groups of people laughing and socializing. Most of the women were dressed like me, except for a few who wore far less clothing. One girl, who appeared to be about my age—but whose true number of years I would never be able to guess—was wearing so little that I actually blushed when she looked at me. She smiled at Albert, but he ignored her. In the distance, I saw a large stone mansion that looked at least several centuries old.

Lots of people were staring at us. This seemed to happen everywhere we went in the supernatural world. Everyone wanted to see the famous Albert Jefferson and his new, only-average wife. I felt self-conscious; many of the men were staring at me, too. I found that particularly strange and uncomfortable. Albert made a low, barely-audible grunting sound in his throat and pulled me closer.

"On second thought," he whispered, "the fishnet tights were not a good idea, and I should have gotten you a longer dress."

I rolled my eyes but decided not to reply.

A tall, fair-skinned man with shaggy black hair and a

thick, neatly-trimmed beard approached us. He was wearing jeans, a suit jacket, and nothing more. He had a girl on each arm. One had long, silky red hair and wore a skin-tight, black leather dress that only reached the top of her thigh. The other had a heap of blond curls that fell down to her chest, concealing most of what her low-cut dress didn't. Their attire wasn't particularly shocking, though. What really surprised me was that they were both...human.

The man gave us a—or, more accurately, Albert—a wide grin. He seemed to blow me off as if I were nothing more than a slightly cute puppy. The girls on either arm didn't appear to notice us at all. They were too busy staring at him. I shrunk against Albert, and his grip on my hips tightened.

"Albert, it's good to see you again," the man said.

Albert nodded and gave him a polite smile. "Same to you, Mars."

Mars gave him another grin. "Enjoy the party."

Albert nodded. "Thank you."

Without a single look toward me, Mars walked away. I relaxed a little bit against Albert. He pulled me tightly toward him with his front to my back. We moved a little ways away from the sea of people before he relaxed.

"The girls, they're human," I whispered.

He sighed. "They want to be turned."

"Oh," I mumbled.

"I'm sorry, Anne," he whispered. "I had been under

the impression that none of his — partners — would be here."

"Have you been to one of these before?" I asked.

Albert stiffened. "It was a long time ago before I met you."

I took his hand in mine. "Hey, it's okay. I was just curious."

He smiled down at me. "You're my everything."

I grinned. "I know."

Albert placed a soft kiss against my lips before pulling me against his chest. He held me in silence for a few moments. I let my body mold into the curves against his, simply relishing in his scent.

"Why didn't Mars look at me?" I asked.

Albert continued to place kisses on my cheeks while he responded. "Mars was born in Rome. He's still...very patriarchal. He knows you're my wife, so he either respects you enough not to look at your physical...attributes or just wasn't interested in your personality."

"Oh," I mumbled.

He looked into my eyes, and I stared back into his dark, stormy sea. I would never tire of looking at him. Under his white dress shirt, I could see the outline of his hard abdominal muscles. His skin was flawless, and his smile could have charmed a temptress. Somehow, he was mine. That was something I would never be able to fully understand.

"I'm sorry, I thought the party would be classier," he

said with a regretful smile.

I lightly traced the outline of his collarbone. "Let's just go home. I'd rather be alone with you."

He smiled. "Are you sure? You were alone with me all day."

I grinned. "It's our honeymoon."

His eyes lit up as he took my hand and led me toward the horses. "You are absolutely right."

Chapter Thirteen
DANCING IN THE DARK

The moon was high in the sky when we arrived back at the cottage. Rays of light from its luminous glow seemed to stream down from the heavens like silver ribbons. They shimmered down from the sky in an alluring way that made my eyes grow wide. I pondered what was beyond, what lay past the stars and beyond the known. The night was peaceful, almost silent.

Joseph met us outside to take the horses. He gave me a soft smile, which I returned. Albert took my hand and helped me down from the carriage. I patted the horses softly and kissed each of them on the neck before Albert gave the reins to Joseph.

"I'll be right back," Albert said before following Joseph toward the barn.

I watched them for a few moments with a smile on my face. Albert looked at ease; that was rare. Sometimes, I saw a glimpse of the way he had been as a boy. But his carefree moments weren't part of our everyday life and usually only lasted for a few minutes. Scotland seemed good for him—as if the clean air made him more at peace with himself.

I made my way into the house and toward the bathroom. After abandoning my blazer, ditching my heels, and washing my face, I walked toward the bedroom in search of a nightgown. But when I opened the door, my jaw dropped.

Sitting on our bed was a gorgeous young woman with long, straight blonde hair that fell to her hips. She had a tiny waist with a wide chest and graceful legs. Her eyes were a bright blue, almost the same color as mine. She had rosy red lips and slightly pink cheeks. Apart from a short, silk slip of a dress that barely reached her thighs, she was completely exposed. For a moment, I marveled at how much she looked like a Barbie doll.

Her eyes met mine in shock; she clearly had not expected me. Well, I hadn't expected her either. I just stared with my mouth open, unsure of what I was supposed to do. It felt as if my heart was running a marathon. I couldn't even guess who she was and wasn't sure I wanted to know. I doubted she was there to see me.

"Who are you?" she whispered.

Suddenly, the bedroom door opened. Albert was beside me, staring at the blonde beauty with a dropped jaw. She was looking between the two of us as if she couldn't figure out what was going on. I was just as confused, but since Albert could see her too, that meant she wasn't a figment of my imagination. This woman in my bedroom was very real.

"Sophie, what are you doing here?" Albert asked with shock plainly audible in his voice.

Sophie scrunched her eyebrows. "I came to see you. I didn't know —"

"Leave," Albert whispered.

She stood from the bed, retrieved a pair of white platform heels, and casually walked past me all the way out the front door of the house. When we heard the door shut, Albert and I stood in silence for a few minutes. Finally, I managed to calm myself. Neither one of us wanted to be the first to talk.

"Who is she?" I asked.

He sighed, "An old...acquaintance. I'm sorry, Anne. She must have found out where I was staying but clearly didn't know about you."

I sat on the bed, carefully pulling my hair from its hold and brushing it out. "How did you know her?"

Albert slid his shoes off and sat beside me. "Do you really want to know?"

I bit my lip. "Probably not."

He ran a hand through his hair. "I met her in 1900. She was a nurse—a human—and we were introduced by a mutual friend. When she was twenty, she became extremely ill. Her life was in danger, and she begged me to save her. I didn't know what else to do. She was the first person I ever changed."

I nodded. "How long?"

He pursed his lips. "I stayed with her for a year, but she wanted to return to Scotland. We parted ways as friends."

Part of me wanted to resent him. But I couldn't because he had been entirely lost. His life before our relationship had been crazy, chaotic, and thrilling. And yes, sometimes it bothered me. But I loved him, and that was what I found most important.

I gave his hand a little squeeze. "It's okay, Albert. We both have pasts. We knew that when we married."

He gave me a soft kiss. "I stopped blaming myself for my history when I met you, Anne. Sometimes, it still haunts me. But when I look into your eyes, I don't regret it. Because everyone I was with, everything I did, led me to you. You need to forgive yourself for everything, Anne. It's not your fault that James died, and it's not your fault that Arthur died, either. You never meant for any of that to happen. You are the kindest, most loving person I know. No one blames you for what happened. If you let go, things will become easier."

"It's not easy to forget," I whispered.

He pulled me into his arms. "You'll never forget, baby. It'll always be there. But you can still live, enjoy life, and be happy."

"I want to feel safe again," I mumbled into his chest.

Albert placed a kiss on my forehead. "One day, little dove. One day, you will. Until then, I won't leave your side."

"How do we survive until that day comes?" I whispered.

He slipped his suit jacket off and unbuttoned his shirt, so my cheek rested directly against his chest. Albert tangled his fingers in my hair and began playing with my curls. I felt his cool, strong wedding ring against my bare skin. He was mine, always. My love for him was stronger than the moon's hold on the tide. There was nothing that could pull me away from him. This depression and melancholy sadness weren't enough to make me want to leave his side. No force could stop the setting of the sun or me from loving my dark, handsome husband. We were like fireflies in the night, dancing in the dark with only our own light to illuminate the black sky.

He tilted my head to meet his and planted another sweet kiss on my lips. "We do this, baby. We do this."

Chapter Fourteen
SURPRISE

The bubbles were perfectly pink and smelled like apple blossoms. My black curls were sprawled around me like streaks of midnight in a flower-filled field. The room was filled with the scent of roses and honey. Soft music was playing in the background, and I focused on the gentle lull of the piano. It was by far the most relaxing bath I had ever experienced.

The door opened, and Albert stepped into the room. He smiled down at me with nervousness in his eyes. I gave him a puzzled look as he handed me a towel. As I began to dry my face, he spoke.

"There's someone here to see you," he said.

I stood and wrapped the towel around me. "Who?"

He pursed his lips. "She wouldn't tell me her name."

Oh no, who could it be? There was no one I knew that Albert didn't. I had no friends that were separate from his. Whoever this girl was, I had no idea where she was from.

I raised my eyebrows. "She isn't one of your exes that you maybe...forgot, is she?"

He shook his head. "No, I've never seen her before."

I sighed. "Alright, I'll be out as soon as I get dressed."

Albert gave me a light kiss on my lips before handing me my robe. He smiled, left the room, and closed the door behind him. In a hurried rush, I grabbed a pink cotton dress and quickly slipped it on. After pulling my wet curls into a ponytail, I sprayed some of the ridiculously expensive perfume Albert had given me on my wrists. I tucked a flyaway piece of hair behind my ear and left the bathroom to meet the mystery woman.

She sat across from Albert in the living room with an anxious smile. The girl appeared to be maybe sixteen years old, but she was a vampire, so I couldn't be sure. She was stunningly gorgeous and almost as beautiful as a renaissance figure. Her eyes were dark brown and complimented her golden hair. She had dark red lips that seemed too heavenly to be real and fair skin. The dress she wore was forest green with small, golden accents. It fell just below her knees to meet the top of her tall, black boots. She was the perfect example of an alluring, picture-worthy vampire to be written about in a novel.

As soon as the girl saw me, she rose and extended her hand. I took it and gave it a soft, friendly shake. Her anxiety seemed to vanish as excitement spread over her features.

"We haven't met," I said, "I'm Anne."

The girl smiled. "My name is Nellie Emerson, and I've been waiting a really long time to meet you."

There was a slight pause before I regained my sense of calm. "Um, please, sit down."

Nellie gave me a big, open grin as I sat beside her. "It's so good to finally see you in person. I've been waiting decades for this."

I raised my eyebrows. "I'm not sure I completely understand."

Albert was sitting in the corner of the room, watching us with a passive curiosity. I gave him a puzzled glance, but he simply shrugged his shoulders.

Nellie took my hands in hers. "I'm your sister, Anne."

I gave a little laugh before pulling away. "I don't have a sister."

Her eyes looked wounded. "You never knew I was born. We don't have the same mother."

My jaw dropped. "Impossible," I whispered.

She shook her head. "After you disappeared, our father had an affair. He fell in love with my mother. When she told him she was pregnant, he paid her to keep me a secret and leave Georgia. I was born in South Carolina and turned into a vampire in 1971. I worked hard to find you but only discovered where you were when I heard about your marriage to Albert. I've been in France for the last ten years.

You were a very difficult person to locate, Anne."

Albert was entirely frozen. He had a look of shock on his face. Apparently, she hadn't told him any of this. We exchanged a nervous glance. This was impossible. My father would have never done that to my mother; they had been married for years before having me. Both of my parents had been devout Catholics. They had been so in love.

She sighed. "I knew you wouldn't believe me, so I brought this."

Nellie handed me a folder with papers inside. I took out the first one and examined it. After reading it, I closed my eyes. It was a DNA test; Nellie was indeed my sister.

Albert stood to take the papers from me. I gave them to him with a shaking hand. Nellie sat quietly as she waited for my reply. What was I supposed to say? I had just discovered that not only did I have a sister, but she was also a vampire. My father had had an affair after my death, and the product was sitting beside me.

"I assume you're upset," she whispered.

I shook my head. "Not with you. It's not your fault."

Nellie nodded. "I understand. It must be a shock."

I laughed. "Yes, it certainly is."

Albert was carefully reading the whole report and paying little to no attention to us. I had no idea what to say to her or what she expected. I was probably her only living relative. But up until moments ago, I hadn't known she existed. Part of me felt guilty, but another resented my father. He had been cruel to my mother — his wife — as well as Nellie's mother. Now we were in a mess I had no idea how to resolve.

"I was hoping that maybe we could get to know each other. You're my only living relative. I understand if you don't want to call me your sister, but maybe we could be friends," Nellie said.

I attempted to appear as cheerful as possible. "Of course."

Her face lit up. "Wonderful! Would you like to go out tonight?"

Trying to hide my still overwhelming shock, I nodded. I had to be nice to her. She had put so much effort into finding me. It wouldn't be right to send her away.

She gave me a huge grin before standing up. "I'll be back at six o'clock."

I stood and followed her to the door. "I can't wait."

She gave me a tiny wave before heading down the walkway. With relief, I closed the door as quickly as possible. Albert was sitting on the couch, looking surprised yet composed. I slumped down beside him, leaning back and staring at the ceiling.

"Well, that wasn't what I had expected," Albert said as he wrapped his arms around me.

I stroked his hair as he pulled me against his chest. There was a pause where all we could hear was each other's breathing and the slight howl of the wind outside. He took a deep breath before pulling me onto his lap.

"Are you okay?" Albert whispered.

I bit my lip. "Well, I'm a little shocked."

He nodded. "As expected."

I cuddled in closer to him. "I don't know what I'm supposed to do. What should I say to her? I have no idea who she is."

Albert took a moment to form his response. "I truly don't know, little dove. I don't know."

Chapter Fifteen
OPEN EYES

The room was lightly lit as I examined myself in the mirror. My black curls were exploding around me like a hurricane of dark, stormy waves. I wore a crimson, skin-tight dress that ended just above my knees and black tights. My shoes were a pair of sparkly platform heels that were fit for anything from a late-night party to a royal ball. At least they made me feel somewhat confident.

Drinks with my sister — what a strange concept. Less than five hours ago, I had no idea that Nellie even existed. Suddenly, I had a biological sister. And she was a vampire, too. What was the chance of that?

Albert sat on our bed reading one of his books on Scottish history. He was very focused, and I had been trying not to disturb him. Albert wasn't going out with us tonight; he thought it was best for Nellie and me to talk alone. I disagreed, but I didn't want to argue with him. For some reason, Albert seemed to think my long-lost sister would be good for me. I wasn't so sure about that. She made me anxious.

In fact, when I was around Nellie, I got a sick feeling in my abdomen. Maybe it was just the shock, but she made me uncomfortable. I wasn't looking forward to seeing her, and I didn't know why she was so determined to have a relationship with me. It was strange. Yes, we were blood relatives. But honestly, she knew nothing about me other than who my father was and that I was married to Albert. It just felt...odd. This was very sudden.

A knock sounded on the door, and I went to answer it. Nellie stood in front of me with her flawless, golden hair and pretty, plump lips. Her eyes were filled with an excitement I simply couldn't understand. She wore a short, black dress that complimented her figure. Her jewelry looked priceless. Around her neck was a golden chain with over a dozen emeralds dangling from it. I didn't even want to imagine how expensive it had been. But where had she gotten it? There was so much about her that made me uneasy.

"I like your necklace," I said while attempting to conceal my suspicious thoughts.

For a moment, I thought I saw a flicker of worry in her eyes. But it was gone in less than a second. Maybe it was my imagination.

Nellie smiled. "Thank you, it was a gift."

I raised my eyebrows before stepping outside and

closing the door. "Oh? From a man?"

"Um, from a friend," she stuttered.

No, I was definitely right. Nellie was hiding something, and I wanted to know what it was. Who would have given her such a valuable necklace if not a partner? It looked to be the price of a small house. I couldn't imagine who would have simply gifted it to her. She had some powerful friends, but who were they? I needed to know. And besides, if it truly was just an innocent gift, why would she hide who it was from? She clearly knew someone she didn't want me to know about. I shuddered at the thought that maybe it was another one of Albert's ex-flings.

When we reached Nellie's car, my jaw dropped. I didn't know what kind of vehicle it was, but I could tell it was expensive...really expensive. I was accustomed to seeing Albert with these types of things; he was an ultra-rich business owner. He worked crazy hours to accumulate his wealth while also providing hundreds of jobs to vampires and werewolves around the world. But Nellie, she wasn't buying these things for herself. Someone was buying them for her, and I was going to find out who it was.

"Nice car," I remarked.

She gave me a tight-lipped smile. "Thanks."

We both sat down in our seats, with her driving and me on the passenger side. Once we reached the main road, I decided it was time to investigate. I had never been particularly good at subtle questioning, but I would do my best. Nellie had regained her sunny composure, so maybe she would start to open up a little bit more.

I attempted a smile. "So, you've been in France?"

Her eyes brightened. "Yes! I love it there. It's beautiful. I was mainly in the countryside but spent some time in Paris, too."

"I wonder if we have any of the same friends. Who were you with in France?" I asked.

She bit her lip. "Oh, I don't think so. I mostly keep to myself."

Her story wasn't adding up. If she had spent most of her time alone, how had she managed to acquire rich friends? Whoever this person was, she certainly wanted to keep it a secret.

"No coven?" I asked.

She shook her head. "Never found anyone interested in starting one. I spent some time drifting through a few larger ones, but they had too many rules."

I pursed my lips. "Rules?"

She gave a little laugh. "Oh, I forgot. You're a vegetarian. Most covens don't drink from humans, either. That all seems so strange to me."

My jaw dropped. "What? You kill people?!"

Well, this was starting to make more sense. If she was going around killing people, she was probably doing other evil things, too. The big mystery was, what was she doing?

She rolled her eyes. "Please, don't start. I have no need for a lecture from my big sister. I'm a vampire. This is what I do."

"Stop the car," I said.

Nellie pulled off the main road into a small clearing. The sun was setting in the sky, and the world was beginning to come alive with the fresh, cool air of the night. But all I could think about was that my long-lost sister was killing people. Just like James, but with a more elegant style. That made it worse, too. She wasn't openly acting like a barbarian; her brand of murder was more inconspicuous.

What was it about the people in my life that made them reckless murderers? For starters, one of the loves of my life had become a homicidal psychopath after turning into a vampire. Then, my sister-in-law had taken up murdering infants. Now, one of my actual blood relatives had just revealed her own homicidal tendencies. Did vampirism make everyone lose their minds? Albert was still sane, but maybe he was just special. Me? Well, there was my little hallucination problem. But at the very least, I wasn't murdering people.

Nellie looked over at me. "Anne, you're a good person. I'm really sorry about this, but I made the deal before I even met you. It was too good to pass up. Again, I am sorry."

Before I could respond, she was out of the car and had long gone into the woods. I didn't have much time to think, though. Moments later, the windshield shattered. I screamed as the glass rained down over me. My ears began ringing, and I could feel the tiny shards pressing into my skin. I was just glad they weren't splinters of wood; that would have hurt much more. Without a second thought, I shoved the door open and tumbled out onto the grass.

"Well, well, well," Hazel announced, "what a dramatic start to the night. It's almost as if I wrote the script myself. Oh wait, that would be because I did."

I struggled to get onto my feet. When I did, Hazel was before me and looking as stunning as ever. She wore a dazzling golden dress that hugged her curves and revealed a large part of her chest, and her hair was glossy and well-combed. Apparently, murder missions were a fancy occasion. Hazel always looked like a fashion designer, though.

"How?" I whispered.

She smirked before replying, "Well, I had some help. You see, Anne, getting almost anything you want is possible if you're willing to pay for it. I bribed some old friends, seduced a few men, and even recruited her," Hazel motioned toward Sophie, "to help me."

I looked at Albert's beautiful ex, now realizing she had never meant to rekindle a relationship with him. The whole thing had been an act. Maybe she had some sick revenge scheme, too. Her whole mission had been to confirm that I was with Albert at the cottage. We had fallen for her little performance. Sophie gave me a sick grin. Apparently, she was just as thrilled about this as Hazel, which definitely wasn't a good sign.

"And," Hazel added, "it was very convenient that I happened to have met your poor, lost little sister five years ago on a trip to the Louvre. Of course, I had no idea how useful she would be. At the time, I had simply been admiring her wardrobe."

"Why would she help you?" I mumbled.

Hazel clucked her tongue. "Oh, so much talking. But if you really want to know, I pay well. Like I said, Anne, money can buy whatever you want. That girl had no real attachment to you. She was simply a very convincing actress. It was helpful that we had the DNA confirmation, though. You wouldn't have believed it without proof."

My heels had sunken into the mud, so I was left standing barefoot with my back pressed up against Nellie's car. Hazel was on my right side, and Sophie was on my left. I wasn't sure which of them was weaker, but I had a feeling they were both stronger than me. They were probably high on human blood, too. That really set the odds in their favor. All I had was some animal blood in my system, hardly more than what was necessary to keep me alive. If I tried to run, they would catch me. If I tried to fight, one of them would kill me. But even if I stalled, no one would come for me. Albert thought I was out having a great night, and no one else —

except for my traitorous sister — knew where I was. It would be hours before Albert even expected something was wrong. By then, I would surely be dead. There was literally nothing I could do.

I looked toward Sophie. "What's your motivation? I never did anything to you. Why do you want to kill me?"

Sophie shrugged. "Hazel paid me well enough to betray pretty much anyone. Besides, the hunt was fun. And you were never good enough for Albert; everyone knows that."

Hazel grinned. "You see, Anne, there are some things you will never come close to understanding. Money and power, they're more important than love. Being feared is the most useful form of acknowledgment, and you ruined that for me on what should have been a very entertaining night. I knew you would be problematic, but I didn't know your overactive, good-girl impulses would make me look weak in front of my entire coven. Ruining your wedding wasn't adequate revenge, so I had to resort to more cunning means of sabotage."

"You really are sadistic," I whispered.

She shrugged. "I don't want your approval. The only good you'll ever do for me is when I can finally announce to the world that I've killed my brother's unworthy wife. After all, no one supports you. All those girls, they're jealous. Not because they want to be you, but because you have what they want—my brother."

Sophie—in all of her Barbie doll beauty—smiled. "So, what do you want me to do? Or do you want to do this part all by yourself?"

Hazel's eyes lit up. "Oh, don't worry. Your part is all done. Albert will never know you had a hand in it. And when she's gone, you might just find yourself consoling my heartbroken brother. You're prettier than her, anyway."

Sophie gave me one last dazzling grin before disappearing into the trees. I glanced back at Hazel, trying to see just how confident she really was. Her eyes were alight with furry, hatred, passion, and excitement. When I concentrated, I could even smell the human blood on her lips. I felt sick to my stomach as my fangs slid free. My base impulses were still there. Sometimes, it was all I could do to not become a monster.

Hazel gave a real, stunned laugh. "See! You are a vampire! I was beginning to wonder if those fangs of yours were even real. You're so well…tamed. It's sickening, really. First, you let that human boy control you. Then, my delusional brother decided he was going to pick up the pieces of your tragic saga. And now, you two live like it's the Middle Ages. It's no longer dangerous to be a vampire, Anne. But we all know the real reason you hide it, you're ashamed of who you are."

My fangs sliced open my lower lip, and I desperately

wanted to cry. This woman, this—evil creature, knew my mind. She seemed to understand me better than I did myself. I missed my mortality, I hated drinking blood, and I truly, desperately wanted to get rid of the guilt that came with being a murderer.

But I loved Albert, and I would never give up on us. He was the only person who had ever accepted every single part of me, and that meant that I could never stop fighting for him. Albert deserved all of my efforts. So until Hazel shoved a dagger through my heart, I would not give up. I had far more to fight for than she did. This was about my husband, my daughter, and refusing to hide from the darkest parts of myself.

I allowed my fangs to become fully exposed, watching Hazel's eyes widen in shock. A moment later, I was on top of her. She ripped her nails against my arm, shredding my skin. I cried out in pain, allowing her to shove me off. Before she could grab a makeshift stake, I grabbed her hair and pulled her backward. She screamed as we tumbled back into the mud, becoming soaked in blood and dirt. Hazel hissed at me, but I lunged at her before she had the chance to move. I held her down, screaming as she drove her fangs into my arm with as much force as she could manage. After a few moments, the pain was too intense. I topped backward, grasping my arm where a huge chunk of flesh was missing. Hazel slapped me across the face as hard as she could, causing my head to bounce back against a rock. My ears began ringing, and my vision started to blur. She was screaming at me, but I couldn't tell what she was saying. *I'm going to die*, I thought. All of a sudden, I felt her being pulled off of me. But when I opened my eyes, everything was blurry.

I couldn't hear anything other than a low, steady buzzing sound that persistently grew louder until it was all I could focus on. The world was going in and out of focus, and I had no idea what was real. Suddenly, a bright, white light overwhelmed me.

When my vision returned, I was back in 1950. I saw Gale dead on the ground, just like the night when I had become a vampire. But this time, I was there with him. We both lay there silently in a puddle of blood. My stomach churned as I looked at our corpses. I had spent innumerable hours imagining this outcome, debating whether or not it would have been better. But now that I truly saw it, I knew it would have been the worst outcome. If I had died that night, I never would have met Albert. Living decades alone had been worth it because I had been able to fall in love with Albert. I had married the love of my life. But if I had died that night, we would have never met each other. It was dark, and seconds later, the image was gone.

Then, I landed back in Savannah, where a human James, lay in a hospital bed. He was pale and looked on the verge of death. James looked maybe thirty years old. On his arms were dozens of scars—needle scars. His face was shallow, his hair torn and bunched in clumps, and his lip dried and cracked. There were bruises on his face and a large cut across his cheek. The doctors were rushing around him, but I could barely hear what they were saying. Machines were beeping so loudly that I was starting to get a headache. Eventually, I managed to catch two words: heart attack. In stunned silence, I watched as his vitals crashed, and he died.

Less than a moment later, I was back at the party where we had saved Penny. But this time, neither Albert nor I were there. Instead, I saw her tiny, helpless body lying lifeless on the table. She was covered in blood with a huge gash on her neck. Her poor, innocent little frame was fractured and broken. She looked like a rag doll–thrown away and ignored. My whole body began to shake. Before I could scream, she was gone.

Then, I watched Anya and a human Arthur kiss in front of a small, pasty-shop window. They looked as happy as ever. I smiled briefly at their bliss. Would their future have been a fairytale? Then, a huge truck slid off the road and crashed into them. It exploded, leaving nothing but a ball of flames and wafts of smoke. I could say nothing, just stare in shock.

"Anne!" Albert screamed.

I opened my eyes to find him above me with a gash on his forehead and blood dripping down his face. Immediately, I panicked. I looked around for Hazel but could find her nowhere.

"Shhh," Albert whispered, "she's dead, Anne. It's okay. You're safe."

I leaned into him, pressing my head against his chest. "How did you find me?"

Albert motioned to his left, where Nellie stood with a grim expression. "She told me."

Chapter Sixteen
YOU ARE MY ALWAYS

"How are you feeling?" Albert whispered.

I was laying on our bed with a drink in my hand as I blindly stared at the news running across the TV. It had been an hour since Albert had brought me back to the house. It was just the two of us. He didn't know what to say, and I didn't, either. We were both just...existing. Remaining calm seemed to take most of my attention; I was still skittish.

"Albert, when you pulled Hazel off of me after I hit my head, I saw these—alternate possibilities. I don't know if it was just my imagination or something else. I hardly question the supernatural anymore. But these possibilities weren't really any better than the way things turned out. They all ended the same way—in death," I said.

There were a few moments where all he did was examine the contemplation in my eyes. Our thoughts seemed to mingle as our souls spoke in a silent dance. Our spirits were connecting with each other, both considering the others' thoughts. Even though I was overwhelmed with confusion, the dark, stormy nature of his eyes pulled me in and consumed my very being.

He took my hands in his. "What do you mean?"

I would never tire of how his touch made my skin come alive. Yes, this whole situation made me scared. It overwhelmed me, but I had him—I had Albert. I didn't really know what to think, yet I was confident he would take care of me. Albert would protect me. Most of all, he wouldn't let my mind get the better of me. I trusted his judgment far more than my own. After all, he was—ironically—the more stable one.

I looked up into his eyes. "I saw myself lying dead beside Gale instead of becoming a vampire. I had imagined it before, but actually seeing it made me realize that I wouldn't have wanted to really die that night. If I had never become an immortal, you and I would have never fallen in love. I saw Arthur, too. If things hadn't happened the way they did, he would have been hit by a truck and died as a human. And I saw James; instead of dying as a vampire, he died of a heart attack without ever knowing me. Of course, I don't know which path he would have chosen. But either way, he would have ended up dead. And this could have just been my imagination. Still, it made me think about us—about everything."

Albert ran his hand gently across my cheek. "No man would ever choose to die without knowing you. Even if it meant I would only get to live a year by your side, I would choose that over spending a thousand years without ever seeing your smile. And, as much as I hated James—because to be clear, Anne, I did loathe him—I know that he would have preferred spending a little time loving you than dying without ever experiencing one of your kisses." Albert placed a soft kiss on my lips. "What else did you see?"

I took a moment before responding. "I saw Penny... covered in blood. She was dead at that party, Albert. Her body was just lying on a table, covered in blood, while they laughed and danced as if nothing was wrong. If we hadn't been there, they would have killed her. And if James hadn't left me, neither of us would have been at the party. If things had turned out differently, we wouldn't be married, and Penny would be dead."

Albert sighed. "The universe has a way of controlling things. Maybe it's fate or destiny, but sometimes things are meant to happen. You couldn't have saved Gale, James, or Arthur. But, Anne, we did save Penny. Because of everything else, she will grow up, and no doubt be a better person than all of us. She was meant to live, and this whole complicated road was the universe's way of ensuring she did."

I leaned back against the pillows. "For a while, I thought I killed them all—that they died because of me.

Maybe it didn't have anything to do with my choices, though. Maybe, as cruel as it sounds, they were just meant to die. I can't explain what I saw, but now I know I wasn't the one who killed them. Even though I did shove a dagger through James' heart, I only did it to save people. He was on a murder spree, and I couldn't just let him keep killing humans. None of the deaths were my doing. They just…happened."

Albert climbed into bed beside me and pulled me onto his lap. "You could never be a villain, Anne. All this time, I've been trying to show you that none of this is your fault. All of these things happened to and around you. You were never the perpetrator; all you have ever tried to do is love people. That's why you're such an amazing woman and one of the reasons I love you."

I leaned back against his chest. "I'm sorry about Hazel. Even though it wasn't my fault, I'm sorry."

He pulled me closer. "It's okay. I was just trying to put it off. She killed more humans than I want to think about, and she had no desire to change. Hazel felt no remorse for murdering innocents. And the moment I saw her about to kill you, I didn't even hesitate. I'm sorry it took seeing your life in jeopardy for me to realize that she was too dangerous to be kept in a cage."

"What about Nellie?" I asked.

Albert shrugged. "I guess she had a change of heart. Of course, when she arrived, I knew something was wrong. Then

I wanted to kill her when she told me what she had done. Clearly, I didn't. She led me back to you, and that's when I killed Hazel."

"I guess my sister is only slightly less psychotic than yours was," I grumbled.

"I'm sorry I didn't see through her. Nellie is a very good actress, though. She deserves an academy award," he grumbled.

I pursed my lips. "How did she even become a vampire?"

"Well, she gave me a story, but I'm not sure if it's true," Albert said. "She claims she fell in love with a vampire, and he turned her. Of course, I asked what had happened to him. She said that he was killed in a fight over something irrelevant. I didn't ask for more details."

"Oh," I whispered.

He pulled me so tightly against him that I could feel every muscle. "I know your transition was far more traumatic than most. It's not fair what that barbarian did to you. I wish you could have chosen it, that you would have known me when you were a human and decided that you wanted this to last forever. But, like you said, if things had happened differently, Penny wouldn't be alive."

I nuzzled my head against his chest. "I don't mind it now, Albert. For a while, I thought what he had done to me had stolen my worth. I felt dirty, as if I could never wash away the filth. Being a vampire seemed like the worst thing in the world. But when I fell in love with you, and you showed me how much you loved every inch of my body, mind, and soul, I realized I was okay with who I am. How I became a vampire doesn't define me. But my love for you, that does. Because my life with you is so much better than anything I experienced as a human. And I don't care that we're not able to do mortal things. I don't care that we're supposed to be miserable because we're so-called 'monsters.' None of that is important because you make me happier than I ever knew was possible."

He took my face in his hands and pressed his lips against mine. For the first time in days, I wasn't distracted by guilt. All I could think about was how beautiful he made me feel and how I loved him far more than my own life. Every cell in my body felt adored by him. Albert loved the darkest parts of who I was, and that made me feel free. I didn't have to hide from him or pretend to be someone else because he was just like me. We were complicated, messy, and so, so blissfully in love.

His hands tangled in my hair as I forgot everything other than him. I let my mind slip away from stress, worry, and fear. When all I could feel was his touch, my pain went away. I felt as if we had left the earth and were surrounded by nothing more than an overwhelming, all-encompassing love. There was light, beauty, and the most amazing man I had ever met. I could see the most dazzling stars, and it was all because of him. Albert was so much more than just my husband and the love of my life. He was my key to understanding who I was meant to be. With him, I felt beyond beautiful.

"You, Anne Jefferson, are by far the most incredible, overwhelmingly amazing thing that has ever happened to me. No matter how long our forever lasts, I will never discover anything more beautiful than you," he whispered.

"I'll love you, always," I mumbled against his lips.

His hands were hard against my back. "And I will always love you, too."

Chapter Seventeen
REHAB

"What are we going to do about Nellie?" I asked.

Albert was sitting at his desk, examining some important documents I hadn't even attempted to understand. His work was something I didn't try to assist with. The business dealings were simply too widespread for me to understand, and Albert wasn't interested in giving up his control. He wasn't consumed with his businesses but rather far too invested to place them in anyone else's hands.

He turned around to face me as I reorganized one of the bookshelves. "I was thinking we could try to—reform her."

I raised my eyebrows. "You want to put her in vampire rehab?"

He nodded. "It's worth a try. After all, she is your biological sister."

I pursed my lips. "How do you plan on conducting

this — therapy?"

Albert gave me a clever grin. "I was thinking we could take her to see Penny."

My jaw dropped. "Nellie will try to kill her, Albert! It would be a disaster."

He shook his head. "I don't think Nellie will hurt her. And if she tries anything, we'll both be there to stop her. I think it will be good for Nellie to see a human she has a familial connection to. Maybe it will make her value mortality. There are no guarantees; I've never tried this before. And trust me, I hate the idea of putting Penny in danger. But at the moment, I can't think of another way to save your sister."

"Nina and Anya are my sisters," I whispered.

He smiled. "I know that, baby. But you and Nellie do have the same father, and in a hundred years, it might be nice to know that there's another person on earth that shares your blood."

I sighed. "Alright, we'll try it your way. But if Nellie so much as looks at Penny with even the tiniest bit of hunger in her eyes, I will shove a dagger through her heart."

Albert grinned. "That's my girl."

~*~

When our bags were packed and ready to go, we said goodbye to Joseph and Becca. I gave carrots to the ponies and promised to bring them more when we returned. I wasn't sure when we would return to Scotland, but I hoped it was soon. It was a peaceful place, somewhere I would feel comfortable taking Penny. Now that Hazel was gone, the cottage was safe. It was hidden away from most of the homicidal vampires roaming the world. If we brought Penny to Scotland, she would be able to have a semi-normal childhood.

Nellie met us at the plane with a skeptical look on her face. When she saw me, she apologized profusely. Of course, I accepted her apologies with as much grace as I could muster. After all, she had saved my life — after leading me to my impending death, that is. Nellie seemed genuinely sorry, though. And since she was willing to return to Savannah with us, I was as polite to her as possible. There was a coolness between us, but that was expected. Albert treated her more like a business acquaintance than a family member, but I was alright with that. He was still more cordial than me, and Nellie didn't mind his professionalism.

Albert became a friendly, overcautious tour guide when we landed in Savannah. On our way back to the complex, he pointed out historical buildings and told Nellie local stories and legends. She seemed fascinated, mostly because this was where I had grown up. I was happy to sit back as Albert managed the conversations. I glimpsed the full extent of his business skills for the first time. I had a feeling that he had probably given this tour before, but never with the stress that his guest might go on a murder spree. It made the whole drive a little more tense.

~*~

As soon as the driver dropped us off at the front door, I dashed through the main floor to the elevator. Albert was right behind me, and Nellie followed us with neutral interest. The ride to the penthouse felt like it took years rather than minutes. When we finally reached the door to our apartment, Albert unlocked it in one swift motion.

She was right there in front of me. When Penny's sparkling eyes met mine, she squealed excitedly and lifted her hands. I picked her up, holding her close against my chest as she cuddled into me. My heart was in my arms, tugging on my hair and playing with my necklace. I breathed in her fresh scent of lavender and baby oil. She was the purpose of my existence. Yes, I was a vampire. And yes, I couldn't have biological children. But some force in the universe, more powerful than I could understand, always had intended for her to be mine — mine and Albert's.

Albert handed the babysitter a stack of cash and closed the door behind her. He joined our embrace, placing a little kiss on Penny's forehead. My whole world was right there. The galaxy seemed dull in comparison to my two favorite people in all of existence. I loved them more than I had ever known a soul could manage. It was as if they were the only source of light in my life. I would burn the world down for them without a second thought. And maybe there was something wrong with that, but it was the truth.

After what seemed like an eternity, I turned around to face Nellie. Albert had his arm around Penny and me, holding us close to his side. Nellie's eyes held both surprise and disbelief. She looked at us as if we were the strangest anomaly she had ever come across. For a few moments, she simply stood and stared at us.

"Nellie," Albert said, "this is our daughter, Penelope Joy Jefferson."

"She's — she's beautiful," Nellie whispered.

Penny turned around to look at her, and their eyes met. She tilted her head to the side, unable to decide whether she could trust this strange, new vampire. Other than the little amount of time she spent with her babysitter, Penny was never with anyone other than Albert, Nina, Anya, and me. She had little experience with strangers, especially ones who looked at her as if she was an unknown creature.

"Would you like to hold her?" Albert asked.

I stiffened, hugging Penny closer to me. Penny didn't understand why I was so tense and began patting my shoulder to let her down. With hesitation, I placed her on the ground. She tottered over to one of her plush dolls, picking it up and tugging on its hair. My eyes flashed between her and Nellie. The tension in my body was stronger than almost anything I had felt before. I wanted to pick Penny up and never let her go.

Nellie stepped away. "I don't want to hurt her. It's

been, well, years since I've ever even seen a baby. I'm honestly not sure if I've ever held one."

Albert smiled. "Don't worry, you won't hurt her. I promise I won't let anything happen."

With hesitancy, Nellie approached Penny. Penny looked up at her with wide eyes, studying her behavior. Nellie was as stiff as a stick, not wanting to get too close. Luckily, she didn't seem to be struggling with blood lust. Her nervousness most came from the unfamiliarity. I had a feeling Nellie would have been more comfortable beside a bloodthirsty tiger.

Nellie knelt down next to her, watching Penny's reaction. Penny looked mostly uninterested; she had apparently decided that Nellie wasn't dangerous. After a few moments of simply ignoring her, Penny handed her doll to Nellie. Nellie's jaw dropped, accepting the doll with shaking hands. Penny tottered away to retrieve another one of her toys. After finding her teddy bear, Penny sat across from Nellie, evidently expecting Nellie to play with her.

Albert watched with an air of satisfaction as Nellie whispered soft words to Penny. She asked her what her bear's name was and if this was her favorite doll. Of course, Penny didn't respond with anything other than incoherent baby talk, but Nellie was still amazed. After a few moments of Penny's relaxed chattering, I began to release the tension I had been holding.

Albert smirked. "It looks like vampire rehab is

working."

I laughed. "As usual, you were right."

Chapter Eighteen
FAMILY CHAOS

The sun was rising in the bright morning sky. It was a clear day with no sign of rain or gloom. I smelled the flowers blooming outside and the salty aroma of the sea. It overwhelmed my senses, bringing with it a cool, fresh sensation against my skin. All of a sudden, I was reminded of how much I loved the ocean. I hadn't been since the wedding, and it was about time we went. Penny loved the water, too. One of my favorite things was watching Albert hold her in the waves. We could take Nellie with us, too.

Nellie was currently staying in one of the apartments on the second floor. She was hardly leaving her room, but Albert was trying to acclimate her to our vegetarian diet. It had been three days since we arrived back in Savannah, and Nellie hadn't had a drop of human blood since leaving Scotland. She was doing relatively well. I was impressed with her progress. Seeing Penny had sparked a new respect for humanity within her. Now, she was practically obsessed with all things related to my daughter. Penny was glad to have a new friend, and I was happy that they were both content.

"So, Nina, Anya, and Roy are coming over tonight," Albert said, "I invited Nellie, too."

But Nina and Anya, I hadn't seen them since Arthur's funeral. I had no idea if Anya would resent me or if she would even acknowledge my presence. She might hate me for Arthur's death. I didn't blame myself for it anymore, but that didn't mean she accepted that his death wasn't my fault.

"Are you sure that's a good idea?" I asked.

Albert walked over to sit beside me on the couch. "Anne, it'll be fine. No one blames you for this. And Hazel is dead, so we can all move on."

I placed my copy of *Gone with the Wind* aside and turned to face him. "I know, Albert. But Anya lost the man she had intended to spend forever with. She hasn't exactly forgotten about it."

He placed a soft kiss on my lips. "She wants to come, trust me. I didn't force her to accept the invitation."

I sighed. "Alright, I trust you."

Albert smiled. "Wonderful, it's time to get ready for a party."

"I hate parties," I grumbled while reluctantly following him out the door.

~*~

The large meeting room on the ninth floor was stocked with drinks and board games and decorated with an array of sweet-smelling flowers and fragrant candles. I hadn't known what to wear, so in the end, I chose a casual, little black dress and sandals. My hair was pulled back into a loose braid, and I wore minimal makeup. Penny was playing with a collection of plush toys that Albert had brought down from her nursery. She looked entirely relaxed. I, on the other hand, was pacing the room like a nervous wreck. Albert was relaxing in one of the plush chairs, casually flipping through a book on economics.

"You know, you really should take it easy," he said.

I rolled my eyes. "I'm trying."

He gave me a small smile. "When they get here, you'll feel better."

I sighed. "I hope so."

Suddenly, the door opened.

Nina came in first, giving me a light kiss on each cheek. "It's so good to see you, Anne. I hope you're feeling better."

I gave her a strained smile. "I am."

After squeezing my hand, she walked over and scooped Penny up in her arms, tickling her and making her laugh.

Roy was next. He took me in his arms, squeezing me tightly. I wrapped my arms around his neck and leaned against him. He softly rubbed my back, placing a light kiss on my forehead.

"We've missed you," Roy said.

I released him from the hug. "I've missed you, too."

He smiled once more before going over to talk to Albert. They engaged in some sort of dull business conversation I decided to ignore.

Then, Anya stepped forward and took my hand. She looked at me with sadness but no anger or resentment. After a moment, she wrapped her arms around me and pulled me close. We stood silently, simply holding each other. All the stress left my body and was replaced by compassion and empathy for my adopted sister. She rested her head against mine, relaxing into our strong embrace. It seemed as if we held each other forever.

"How did you do it?" Anya whispered. "When you lost James, how did you do it?"

I took both of her hands in mine. "I focused on staying alive one second at a time. It was miserable, but you already know that. I didn't handle it well, Anya. You're far stronger than I am."

She smiled sadly. "No, Anne. You've had to deal with so much unjustified guilt. I know you blamed yourself for everything, but I never did. It wasn't your fault, and you don't deserve to be miserable for a death you didn't cause. And besides, Hazel is dead. I feel better knowing that Arthur's murderer died for what she did. At least he was avenged."

"I'm so sorry," I whispered.

She took my face in her hands. "Don't be, Anne. It's not your fault. All everyone keeps telling me is that they're sorry. I don't need to hear it anymore, especially not from you. You've tormented yourself enough."

"If you need anything, all you have to do is ask," I replied.

Anya smiled. "I know, thank you. But what I really want is for everyone to stop treating me like a skittish animal. Too many people are acting like I'm an orphaned child. I don't want to be without him, but I don't have a choice. So, I'll be okay."

"You're not alone, Anya. I just want to make sure you know that," I whispered.

She wrapped me in her arms. "I do. And believe me, I'll ask if I need anything."

"Hey, you two, come over here!" Albert shouted. "We're setting up Monopoly, and I plan to win."

Anya rolled her eyes. "Coming!"

~*~

Somehow, the game lasted three hours. Predictably, Albert won. I was the least successful player, which wasn't even a bit shocking. Nina was a close second, but Albert managed to win at the last moment. It had been years since I'd played Monopoly.

At the end of the game, I realized that someone was missing. Nellie had never shown up. As Albert was cleaning up the board, I tapped his shoulder. There was no way her absence was a good thing.

"Albert, Nellie never came," I whispered.

He pursed his lips. "I forgot about that. She didn't message me, either. That's not a good sign."

No, it was a very bad sign. Maybe Nellie had decided that a vegetarian diet wasn't for her and found some poor, innocent human to feed on. There could be a dozen people dead by now. Why had I actually believed that she could be reformed?

"Where's your phone?" I asked.

"Dead," he replied.

I pursed my lips. "Mine, too."

Anya was playing with Penny, and Nina and Roy were debating which game to play next. They wouldn't notice if we slipped out for a few seconds.

"I think we should check her room," Albert said.

"Let's go," I replied.

We silently left the room, making our way down to the elevator. When we arrived at Nellie's floor, we dashed down the hall. Anxiety coursed through me as I anticipated what we might find. But when we arrived, I was met with an unexpected sight. Her door was wide open and stained with blood. My jaw dropped as I stared at it in disbelief.

"Well, that's not good," Albert said.

We carefully entered the room, making sure there was

no one inside. The furniture was broken and smashed. Blood was on the walls and the carpet, leaving a trail of red all over the space. I saw no signs of her or anyone else. It was clear that some sort of conflict had occurred. I just wasn't sure what it had been about.

It wasn't human blood, though. All of these stains and chaos, both literally and figuratively, smelled of vampires. There wasn't even the slightest scent of a human in the room. This was not due to Nellie going on a killing spree. It was the scene of a kidnapping.

"Look at this," Albert said.

He held up a small piece of paper left on the coffee table — which was miraculously still stable. I took it from him, examining the scribbled handwriting. My stomach lurched inside my abdomen.

My dear Albert,

I hope you're well. Of course, by now, I'm sure you've discovered that your sister-in-law is missing. Don't worry. She's relatively unharmed. Though, she did put up a good bit of resistance. This girl, Nellie, really isn't all that special. In fact, she reminds me of her sister in terms of her lack of uniqueness. She won't be alive for much longer. You see, I was hoping to rekindle the romance between us. You're the only man I've ever loved, and I know I'm better than that uncivilized American wife you've acquired. She's just a plain girl with nothing notable about her. Your wife doesn't understand the world you're from. She'll never live up to the title of 'Mrs. Jefferson'. You don't deserve to be held down by the silly, mortal notion of marriage. It's too mundane for you. Albert, you're a king and deserve to be treated like one. I'm hoping that this will pull you out of your delusions of domesticity.

With undying love,
Sophie

"Abduction seems to be rising in popularity," Albert grumbled.

We were silent for a moment. What Sophie said about me — what many of the women in Albert's circles said about me — stung. I wasn't from his world. I was just a normal, typical girl from Georgia. There was nothing about me, aside from my immortal body, that made me particularly attractive. I wasn't a beauty queen. In fact, I was a far cry from the other girls Albert had been in relationships with. But I was his wife, and that gave me a small bit of confidence.

"You have terrible taste in women," I mumbled.

"Excluding you, I'd have to agree," Albert said.

"So, what do we do?" I asked.

He sighed. "We resort to the only sure methods of persuasion: violence and blackmail."

Chapter Nineteen
ALRIGHT

Albert employed the most skilled werewolf trackers to locate Nellie. They were part of Roy and Arthur's old pack and more than willing to help hunt down a renegade vampire. Since Sophie wasn't familiar with the area, there was no specific place she might go. In fact, this was her first time in America. We had no idea where to look. But with four werewolves scouring the city and surrounding areas, we received information surrounding their location within an hour.

I still wasn't sure how I felt about Nellie. I didn't trust her, but she also didn't deserve to die. We had brought her to America, so it was our responsibility to ensure she stayed alive. And Nellie had been willing to try a vegetarian diet, which did make me more sympathetic toward her. Besides, her abductor was Albert's crazy ex-girlfriend, which made it even more of our problem. Sophie was trying to get back at us. She had nothing against Nellie. It was our job to deal with her.

"I'll keep Penny," Anya said.

We returned to the party to tell Roy, Nina, and Anya

what was going on. They all had grim expressions, but they weren't panicking. I didn't want them to feel obligated to help. Still, they seemed eager to assist.

"Are you sure?" I asked.

She nodded. "Yes, you need to go save her."

They didn't even know Nellie. In fact, they had never met her. But Nina and Anya — being the best kind of vampires in existence — wanted to save her, even though they had no personal motivation. Immortality was good for some people. On occasion, it brought out the best parts of an individual's personality. Nina and Anya were two examples of that.

"And we'll go with you," Nina said.

I sighed, glancing around the room filled with board games and cards. It had been such a fun night. Well, not anymore. Now it was time to go deal with another homicidal psychopath. I wanted some sort of certification. Maybe I could be an honorary psychologist — if that title even existed. I certainly knew enough about personality problems.

Penny was eyeing us with confusion. She had enjoyed spending the night with all of her family. Penny didn't get nearly enough time spent doing normal, human things. I wanted to change that. Not until all of her father's crazy acquaintances were gone, though. Until then, Penny would have to stay locked in her ivory tower.

"Alright, let's go," Albert said.

~*~

We drove for over an hour out into the woods. It was a dark, wet night, and the moon was covered by stormy clouds. I shivered, not from the cold but rather due to the eerie atmosphere. There was a chill in the air, yet I wondered if it was from my imagination. When we reached the address, there was nothing other than trees.

"That's not what I was expecting," Nina said.

Albert frowned. "Time to walk."

Ugh, I thought.

I felt the mud squish under my black combat boots as we made our way through the woods. My jacket was damp from the few raindrops that were falling, and my curls were stuck to the back of my neck. I felt disgusting, to say the least. Why did it seem like all kidnappers picked the middle of the woods as their chosen arena? It certainly made me feel even less helpful — I wasn't exactly an outdoors expert. Other than Roy, we were all a little out of our element. The four of us were entirely silent; the only thing audible was the sound of a few nocturnal creatures rustling in the woods.

Roy was evidently missing his werewolf tracking abilities. The inability to turn seemed to be the only thing he truly hated about being a vampire. I couldn't imagine having the ability to transform into an animal. But to him, it had been second nature. Now, he couldn't pick up on a scent any better than the rest of us.

Nina was carefully following behind me, paying close

attention to every little detail of the night. Her eyes wandered over everything from the tall, mysterious trees to wet blades of grass. I could sense her anxiety. Mine was heightened, too. Neither of us were fighters. Nina was a bleeding heart, and I preferred avoiding conflict. Still, our natural tendencies weren't going to stop us.

"I feel like I'm in a horror movie," Nina mumbled.

Me too, I thought.

"Don't speak too soon," Albert whispered.

We continued walking deeper and deeper into the dark woods. The further we got, the more it felt like a marsh. My boots were soaked up to my ankles, and water dripped from my face. The rain kept falling harder, and soon it was a heavy shower. I sighed, unable to hold the shiver that had invaded my bones. We were soaked and still hadn't managed to find them.

"Stop," Albert whispered.

Nina, Roy, and I froze, not understanding why. Albert motioned straight ahead, and I saw the faint outline of a barn. The building was falling to pieces, and there didn't seem to be any house around it. The barn was abandoned — a perfect place for hostage holding.

"Listen," Nina said.

When I blocked out the natural sounds of the woods, I heard movement within the barn. But it wasn't from an animal. There was at least one vampire inside. I could tell because she wasn't breathing, just moving. Vampires could choose whether or not to breathe. I normally did it simply out of habit, but I could survive without oxygen. After all, my heart didn't need it; it didn't beat.

"That's her," Albert whispered, "I recognize her scent."

My stomach tightened at the thought that Albert knew what Sophie smelled like. It made me nauseous to think of them together. But of all the girls Albert had ever been with, she probably wasn't the worst.

"What do we do?" I asked.

"We go," Roy replied.

With inhuman speed, he disappeared in a rush toward the barn. Nina took off behind him, and Albert and I followed. Before I reached the door, a large crash that sounded like mountains colliding erupted from within.

When I entered, Roy was holding Sophie up by the neck against the wall. The fury in his eyes made me shiver. He was more filled with rage than I had ever seen him. Roy was taking all of his anger out on Sophie, treating her as the tangible cause of all of his pain. Nina was crouched on the ground beside Nellie, who was unconscious from having her neck snapped. Nellie looked alright, though. Albert rushed toward Roy and Sophie, pulling a stake out from the inside of his black leather jacket.

I was about to look away, but Albert drove the stake into Sophie's chest before I could. Her eyes were filled with shock. She had never expected him to actually kill her. That was clear. Because in the most secret parts of her heart, Sophie believed Albert still loved her. I understood that because I couldn't imagine a world after Albert—a life where I had to live without him. She began fading away, her body turning to small, gray flakes of ash. Then, there was nothing left of her; Sophie was gone.

It happened so fast that I barely had time to process it. In less than a second, Sophie had gone from our biggest threat to nothing at all. She was dead, and I was frozen in disbelief. I couldn't forget the last expression that had ever crossed her face. Her eyes had been filled with such betrayal. Albert didn't even look fazed.

"Nellie won't wake up!" Nina shouted.

Albert and Roy rushed toward her.

After a quick glance, Albert said, "She'll be fine. Let's get home."

Roy lifted Nellie, whose clothes were covered in her own blood, and carried her out into the woods. Nina, Albert, and I followed. There was a new stillness in the air. Everything had become cold, almost icy. Suddenly, the night seemed quiet.

We rode back home in silence. It seemed like a very long car ride. Albert drove with steady hands and distracted eyes. He looked like a statue. Nina was resting her head on Roy's shoulder, and Nellie was still unconscious.

I glanced over at Albert, watching as his mind spun with contemplation. His lips were pursed into a tight line. Anxiety seemed to shroud his face, and for the first time, he didn't seem like a young man. Before we had started our relationship, Albert had been a notorious, rich, immortal bachelor. Now, he was burdened by deeper, darker things. His eyes were more mysterious than ever. Somehow, they seemed more intense than the starless, bleak night sky. His shoulders were filled with tension, and the muscles in his hands were alert. I wanted to calm him, to tell him it would be okay, and to tell him that I loved him. He had given up his life of pleasure for me, and I would never forget that. But in that moment, I was too afraid to speak.

"We're home," Albert said.

All I could do was stare at him, hoping we would be alright.

Chapter Twenty
AND FOREVER

"Albert?" I whispered.

He looked up at me with eyes that seemed older than the world. Albert's hair was a mess, and his face was lined with stress. A pair of cotton sweatpants hung lazily from his waist, and water beads dripped down his chest. Somehow, without even trying, he looked as handsome as ever. But something about his posture, a strange awkwardness, revealed his anxiety. It was a rare occasion when Albert was so thoroughly exhausted. He ran his hands through his hair, glancing up with concern.

"Is something wrong?" he asked.

I shook my head. "Nellie is fine. She woke up and just wanted to be alone. We put her in a new suite until her first one can be repaired. Nina, Anya, and Roy returned to their rooms, and Penny is asleep."

He nodded. "Good."

I took his hand, leading him from the bathroom back to our bed. Our bedroom was lightly lit and smelled of rose petals. We both sat down; neither of us spoke. Albert remained still, simply staring at the floor. This had never happened before. What was I supposed to say? He was completely drained and tired to the point where he couldn't even pretend to be okay. Albert was burnt out. It was something I had never thought possible. Yes, we were immortal. And yes, we had extraordinary strength. Still, we had hearts—even though they didn't beat.

"Is there anything I can do?" I asked.

He looked at me with confusion. "About what?"

"Albert," I whispered, "you're tired. I'm not blind; I can tell that you're hurting. You've been so supportive and helped me through my problems. Now, you're burnt out. It's my time to be there for you."

He gently reached up to touch my hair. I leaned into his hand, allowing him to cup my cheek. His fingers traveled across my jaw, tracing the outline of my face and neck. Albert's touch was more soothing than the most relaxing cup of tea. I loved him more than I knew how to process. There weren't enough words in the whole world to describe my feelings for him. Every single moment, my love for him grew.

"I've never felt so weak," he said.

I took his face in my hands. "Albert, you are not weak. You have been so strong. Everyone gets tired, though."

He looked down. "I don't want to be a burden to you."

Then, I saw him. I saw that sliver of his being that was still a child trying to please. Albert wanted to be stronger than everyone else. He needed success to feel worthy. Like me, he would never feel good enough. And in a situation like this — where he was so thoroughly exhausted — his insecurities came out. I was glimpsing yet another part of my complex husband.

I pulled his body against mine. "You could never be a burden. You are the love of my life, the most important person in my world. I just want you to let me take care of you."

He leaned against my shoulder, relaxing into me. I ran my hands up and down his spine, gently massaging his back. Albert let out a deep breath, placing his head against my chest. I scattered kisses on the top of his wet curls, nuzzling my head against his.

"Just for a few minutes. I'll only rest for a few minutes," he mumbled.

"Alright, baby," I whispered, "just a couple minutes."

I leaned back against the bed, holding him even tighter. Albert didn't speak. I listened to his heavy breathing, marveling at how his very existence made mine worthwhile. We stayed there all night, just holding each other. Neither of us felt the need to utter a single word. Feeling him against me was enough. His presence was plenty for me to focus on. Our legs were tangled together, and our fingers were intertwined.

Eventually, the rest of the world seemed to blur around us. It was just Albert and me—nothing else mattered. Feeling his breath against my skin was one of the most marvelous sensations I had ever known. Feeling his chest expand against mine was one of the rawest, most comforting things I could imagine. All I could focus on was the curve of his shoulder blades and how his muscles rippled in his back. I was entirely consumed with admiring the man I loved more than my own life.

~*~

When the sun began to rise in the sky, Albert sighed. He lifted his head, propping himself up on his elbows. I smiled at him, brushing a stray curl out of his eyes. His face was no longer stricken with exhaustion. Albert looked refreshed—almost relaxed.

"Thank you," he whispered.

I placed a light kiss on his lips. "You don't need to thank me. I'm your wife—this is my job. We said forever, remember?"

His dark, chocolate eyes bored into mine. "Always."

"We're in this together," I replied.

Albert took one of my curls between his fingers and began twirling it around. "I could never do it without you. Anne, you are what keeps me stable. Before you, I was a mess. That time is something I avoid thinking about. Until I met you, I didn't understand love. But now that you're mine, the world seems like a far more beautiful place."

"I still have no idea why you think so highly of me," I whispered.

He looked at me with bewilderment. "Anne, you are the most remarkably beautiful, intelligent, kind, and caring woman I've ever met. I knew I wanted to marry you long before you ever considered loving me. And when I saw how much you care about life—about defending innocent people—I realized that you are far more than ordinary. Little dove, you exceeded all of my expectations. I am more than honored to be your husband. Don't question your worth around me—I won't allow you to think like that."

I laughed. "I'm just the lucky girl who managed to marry Albert Jefferson."

He smiled. "That's where you have it wrong, baby. You're the main event. I'm just the afterthought."

Oh, Albert Jefferson being the 'afterthought.' That was about as possible as the sun being nothing more than a lightbulb. He could never be anything less than the star.

I rolled my eyes. "Mhm, sure."

He raised his eyebrows. "I'll prove it. Just wait and see."

"Oh, I can't wait," I said.

Instead of replying, he scooped me up in his arms and lifted me off the bed. Albert grinned as he carried me toward the bathroom.

I giggled. "What are you doing?"

He smiled. "You are going to take a bath while I prove that I am, above all else, only your husband."

"What?" I asked.

He set me down on the floor before turning on the faucet. I watched as he poured lavender oil into the tub, along with soft, silky soap. Bubbles began to form as the steamy water rose. He had an unmistakable grin on his face.

Albert pointed to the tub. "Take a bath. I'll be back."

I raised my eyebrows. "Okay…."

"Good," he replied.

I watched as he left the steam-filled room. He looked like he was on a mission. I decided not to worry about what it was. After all, when Albert was determined to do something, I couldn't stop him.

Chapter Twenty-One
YOURS

I sat in the living room with my wet curls hanging around my shoulders. My black silk robe was wrapped around me, with my pink nightgown underneath. I mindlessly searched through the selection of shows, trying to find something interesting. Eventually, I settled on Victoria—one of my favorite TV shows.

Penny was still asleep in her nursery, so I pulled a fuzzy blanket over me and waited for Albert to return. I was exhausted, and this was the best thing to do. After taking a long bath, some of the tension had left my muscles. Now, it was time to just zone out on the couch until Albert came back to hold me. I had no idea what he was doing, but I knew he was determined to accomplish it. Albert's grand plans made me nervous; they were normally extravagant.

The door opened, and I heard Albert's footsteps as he approached me. His strong hands rested on my shoulder, gently massaging my upper back. He leaned over to place a kiss on the top of my head, then reached down to grab the remote and turn the TV off.

"Where were you?" I asked.

He sat down beside me, wrapping his arm around my shoulders. I glanced up at him with curiosity, taking a moment to inhale his familiar, comforting scent. Albert had a huge grin—the kind that indicated he had a huge surprise.

He placed a manilla folder in my hands.

"What is it?" I questioned.

Albert's smile grew. "Open it."

And when I did, my jaw dropped. There was a huge stack of papers, all official legal documents. I flipped through a multitude of warranty deeds, each of them dedicated to a separate company, property, or business. One was a café in Miami and another in Istanbul. There was a bed and breakfast in Amsterdam and a fancy restaurant in Edinburgh. I flipped through dozens more papers with a variety of businesses, some rentals, and prosperous companies. The most surprising aspect was that all the property deeds listed my name as the owner.

"What?" I whispered, "Albert, what did you do?"

He smiled as he touched my cheek. "It's all yours, baby. I needed you to know that you're my everything. This was the best way I knew to convince you."

"Albert, I have no knowledge about business. I'll run

them into the ground!" I said with panic in my voice.

He laughed. "Don't worry, little dove. You don't need to do anything. I'll still run them. But on paper, they're yours.

"But Albert, I don't want any of these," I whispered. "I never wanted you for your money."

He took the folder from me and placed it to the side. "I know, but this is what I wanted to do. Without you, it's nothing, Anne. All of the money, it would be irrelevant if I didn't have you. At this point, I don't even know if I could live without you by my side. You are my motivation. These are yours because they always have been. Now it's just on paper. It's simply another way to say 'I love you.'"

I shook my head. "I can't believe you. This is totally over the top."

He laughed. "Anne, I can't stop myself when it comes to you. There's no hope for me. I'm yours, body, heart, and soul."

"Are you sure?" I whispered.

"Anne," Albert replied, "I have no doubts. You're the love of my life. There's nothing I wouldn't give you."

"I don't know what to say," I whispered into his chest.

He wrapped his arms around me and nuzzled me close. "Don't say anything, baby."

This man was beyond belief. He would always strive to prove himself to me. Maybe that was part of why I loved him. Even though I was totally his in every way, he kept pursuing me. Albert refused to simply accept that I adored him. I couldn't understand why. He was completely deserving of love. Still, he never stopped trying to win my affection. Maybe that was why my love for him grew every second of every minute of every day. Eventually, he would learn how much I loved him.

"I love you," I said.

"I love you, too," he replied before bringing his lips to mine.

Chapter Twenty-Two
MEETING YOU

"Anne?" Nellie whispered.

I was standing in Penny's nursery, cradling her against my chest, and she sucked on her bottle. The lights were turned low as Beethoven played in the background. Other than the soft music, the room was silent. Penny was swaddled in a pink blanket, almost ready for her nap. I rocked her carefully, wanting her to fall asleep.

"Yes?" I replied.

"Can I come in?" Nellie asked.

I nodded.

She entered the nursery, closing the door behind her. "I wanted to talk to you."

"What about?" I asked.

Her eyes turned soft. She wore a pair of tight jeans, a sweatshirt, and tennis shoes. Her hair was pulled into a bun, looking casual and relaxed. She appeared alright, considering she had survived a kidnapping and assassination attempt.

"I wanted to thank you," she said.

I gave her a small smile. "It's not a big deal. You saved my life, so we saved yours."

She bit her lip. "You didn't give up on me, though. You brought me back to Savannah. You let me be around Penny, helping me realize the value of mortality."

We both paused for a moment. I didn't know what to say. She was so sincere. There had been a time when I hadn't believed that vampires could change. I had been convinced that some people were just incapable of dealing with immortality. But Nellie, she had restored some of my faith in our species. Sometimes, people were able to change.

"I'm glad that I did," I said. "But, it was Albert's idea."

She laughed. "Yeah, I guessed that. You're very lucky. He's a great guy."

I smiled. "I know."

Nellie smiled down at Penny. She signed a look of longing displayed on her face. "I regret changing."

My eyes grew wide. "What?"

"I regret becoming a vampire," she said. Sadness flooded her eyes. "I used to think that I never wanted a baby. After being born to a single mother and learning that my father didn't care that I existed, I grew up with a certain disdain for happy couples. Maybe that's why I've never had a good relationship. But seeing you with Penny makes me think about what could have been."

I was filled with sympathy for her. "I'm so sorry."

She shook her head. "It's alright. You were the one who didn't decide to become a vampire. You wanted to stay human, I didn't. You deserve to live a little of the life you wanted."

"Still," I whispered.

She smiled. "It's alright, Anne. Maybe one day I'll be as happy as you. Though, there's certainly not another man as amazing as Albert."

I laughed. "You're right. There's not."

She paused. "If you could change it, would you? Being a vampire."

I stared down at Penny, watching as her eyes slowly closed. Her little finger slid from the bottle as her breathing slowed. I gently took it from her and lowered her into her crib. She reached for her stuffed bear, cuddling against it. Penny was the most beautiful thing I had ever seen. She was like a flower blooming in the spring. Penny was my little angel. She had saved me.

"No," I whispered, "I wouldn't have chosen anything else. This was the life I was meant to live. I was destined to be a vampire, even if it wasn't what I originally wanted. This is where I'm meant to be."

I was incredibly lucky to have Albert and Penny. They were exactly what I wanted. I was the only vampire in history—that I knew of—to adopt a baby. Even though I hadn't carried her, she was my little girl. I was meant to be her mother.

Nellie smiled. "I can see that."

"You'll be happy, too," I said. "Eventually, you'll discover what you're meant to do."

She nodded. "You're right. One day, I'll meet him."

I walked toward her and took her hand in mine. "You'll find someone. The right man is out there. You're just not meant to meet him yet."

She wrapped her arms around me. "I'm glad I met you."

I hugged her back. "I am, too."

Chapter Twenty-Three
FOR A WHILE

Nina and Anya sat beside me on two bar stools. It was the first time I'd been out with them since adopting Penny. Albert and Roy stayed home with her while Nina, Anya, and I had some alone time. They had insisted we go out. It was nice to be with them again, just the three of us spending some time together.

As usual, the club, which I now owned, was noisy and filled with people. Music blared, and sparkles flew around the room as they reflected off the sequins on some of the girl's shoes. It was noisy, but I didn't really mind.

Nina wore a short black dress that hugged her chest but blossomed into ruffles when it reached her waist. Her hair was sleek and shiny, complimenting her minimal makeup. Nina's eyes were bright with excitement, her lips plump and round, almost the color of cherries. I hadn't seen her so dressed up since the wedding.

Anya was wearing a scarlet lace dress. It fell down to her knees, highlighting the most gorgeous parts of her form. Her curls were neatly combed and laid across her back, and her eyelashes were thick and dark. She looked like the most beautiful woman in the room.

"I have something to tell you," Anya said, "I'm leaving."

Leaving? What did she mean by leaving? Had she decided that we weren't a good fit for her? What if Arthur's death had been too much? Maybe she'd found a new family, one that was less complicated.

Nina didn't look surprised at the new information.

I turned toward Anya. "Why?"

She smiled softly. "I need to heal. There's a beautiful getaway in Hawaii filled with tropical plants, flowers, and air. It's safe, calm, and tranquil. I'll only be away for six months."

Only six months. Well, it wasn't permanent. She wasn't really leaving us. This was like a vacation. Anya would be back.

"Are you sure?" I asked.

Anya nodded. "Yes. And I asked Nellie to go with me."

Nellie? Anya was taking Nellie with her? They were not a set of travel buddies I would have put together. They were both alone, though. Maybe it was a good idea.

"Nellie?" I asked.

"She's lonely, too. I thought it might be nice to take her

with me," she replied.

I smiled. "Well, I hope you have fun. Of course, I'll miss you."

Anya smiled. "We will, and I'll miss you too."

"And Roy and I will be going to Spain," Nina said.

What? They were all going away! Every member of my family, other than Albert and Penny, was leaving.

My eyes grew wide. "You're all leaving?"

"Only for a while," Nina said.

"We'll be back," Anya added.

Nina and Anya smiled at me. They were both shining with hope. I didn't want to be separated from them, but it was only for a while. We had served an important role in each others' lives, and we would continue to. Moving to separate parts of the world didn't mean that we would lose contact. After all, we could still call each other. Anya needed to heal. Maybe she, along with Nellie, could do that on the other side of the world. Sometimes it was helpful to leave the place where bad things had happened. I wouldn't blame Anya if she never came back to Savannah. Of course, I wanted to be near her. But I also knew that it was hard for her. She was living in a place filled with memories of Arthur. Everywhere she went brought his death to mind. And Nina and Roy, they deserved to have some time alone. They hadn't really been given that chance because of all the chaos. I loved my family. So until we were all ready to come back together, it was time to let them go. I could be content with the knowledge that they were finding happiness, even if it meant we had to spend some time physically apart.

"We have tonight, though," Nina said.

Anya smiled. "Come on, Anne. Let's have fun."

I glanced back between the two of them. "Alright."

They both took one of my hands, pulling me toward the dance floor.

I enjoyed a few more hours with my best friends. We paid little attention to the music, lights, or other people. It was all about being together. Being with them made me think about how much my life had changed. Yet through it all, Nina and Anya had never given up on me.

~*~

Later that night, we returned home. I watched as they packed their bags. My heart squeezed, but it didn't break. They weren't leaving forever, so I didn't have to say goodbye. Just an hour after we arrived back home, Roy and Nina boarded a private plane and were on their way to Spain. Then, Anya and Nellie left for Hawaii. Before the sun rose, they were all gone.

Chapter Twenty-Four
GETTING BETTER

"So, you're doing better?" Niko asked.

He looked as organized as ever. With his leather journal and sharpened pencil, I almost felt like he was a bird watcher and I was some sort of exotic parrot. Niko smiled at me, though. I was sure that my previous hallucinations had probably terrified him. This was the first time I had seen him since leaving for Scotland. Unlike our previous sessions, this wasn't tense. I didn't feel awkward, and that was a shock. Honestly, I had been expecting the dread to set in about an hour ago, but it never arrived.

"Yes," I said.

"Your hallucinations, they stopped?" Niko replied.

He looked inquisitively at me, almost as if he was trying to read my mind. Well, maybe he was. Niko seemed to know more about my subconscious than me. Perhaps my answers were a secret code he had to transcribe. But the answer was simple.

I nodded. "Yes."

"When?" Niko asked.

I wondered if Albert had already given him all of this information. It would be surprising if he hadn't. Maybe Niko wanted to hear it from me, though.

"After we went to Scotland, and Hazel tried to kill me, I had a vision—or something like that—of alternate possibilities. I'm not sure what happened or what they were, but I saw that I could have done nothing to save James or anyone else. The deaths weren't my fault. They were bound to happen. I don't know why the universe decided that James was supposed to die young, but it did. It wasn't my fault," I replied.

"Interesting. So do you have a takeaway? Any new conclusions?" Niko asked.

"I don't know, but I have realized there's a reason for everything. Nothing happens by accident," I whispered.

Niko smiled. "I couldn't agree more."

Niko paused for a minute, thoughts running through his mind. I could tell he was contemplating something, but I wasn't sure what it was.

"You've made lots of progress, Anne. To be honest, I wasn't sure you were capable of coming so far. I'm embarrassed to say that I doubted your ability to heal, considering all of the pent-up trauma you've carried. But you seem to be on your way to a stunning recovery," Niko said.

I raised my eyebrows. "You doubted your methods?"

He laughed. "I had never before encountered a case such as yours. You were a supernatural, medical mystery. Not to mention a physiological battlefield. I can't explain how much you've surprised me."

"So, is this our last session?" I asked.

He nodded. "It is unless you ever decide there's something else you'd like to discuss."

"I'm surprised you're letting me go," I whispered.

Niko pursed his lips. "Why?"

I sighed. "For a while, I thought you were one step away from locking me in some sort of vampire asylum. I didn't even feel safe from myself. I was sure that you didn't feel safe around me. Besides, like you said, you had never encountered anyone like me before."

Niko shook his head. "Anne, I've had lots of patients that I haven't felt safe around. You are not one of them. Even when you were at your lowest, I could tell you would have done everything in your power to avoid hurting someone else. I was worried that you would injure yourself or worse, but I never thought you would hurt another person without cause."

I smiled. "So you didn't think that I was totally gone?"

He took my hand in his and squeezed it. "Never. I wouldn't have given up on you. I know that you're accustomed to being doubted. Neither I nor Albert would have let you go. We were going to fight for as long as it took. For your sake and ours."

"I thought you only wanted to talk to me for academic reasons," I replied.

Niko raised his eyebrows. "Anne, I have listened and read about your life from the age of seventeen to the present. I couldn't separate my professional curiosity from my empathy. Besides, my job was to help you. You were never a lab rat."

I smiled. "Thank you."

Niko gave me a grin. "It was my pleasure."

Chapter Twenty-Five
AFTER YOU

"So, how did your session with Niko go?" Albert asked.

I smiled as he gently ran his hand along my spine. We were curled up on the couch, watching as *Gone with the Wind* came to a close, and the TV turned off. He placed a soft kiss on my cheek, pulling the blanket tighter around us.

"Good," I whispered.

I could feel his smile. "Does he want to see you again?"

I shook my head. "Not unless I ask to."

Albert gave a satisfied sigh. "Good."

I laid my head against his chest, nuzzling tighter against him. He wrapped his arms around my back. Albert ran one of his hands through my hair, carefully separating the curls, so they fell in an ocean of black around his fingers. He watched me intently, his brown eyes boring into mine. Oh, I loved his eyes.

"Do you remember the first time we met?" Albert

asked.

I smiled. "Yes, it was a long time ago."

He laughed. "I was sure you hated me that day."

Yes, I remembered. It had been a dark winter evening. Nina and Anya had dragged me to a black-tie event. I couldn't even remember what it was for. It was the first overly fancy party I had ever been to. I'd been completely overwhelmed by the number of attendees and their apparel. Of course, Nina had been stunning in an a-line, ruby ball gown with long sleeves and black stilettos. Anya had worn a navy, tea-length dress and a pair of white, high-heeled boots. Since I hadn't known what to wear, I'd chosen a simple, modest, black sheath dress that fell to my knees and a pair of pumps. Moving around the room, I noticed that I was the only one in black. Everyone else wore elegant, extravagant clothes in a variety of colors. I felt awkward, especially since I had no idea who I was supposed to talk to or what to do. Eventually, Nina and Anya both left me to go dance. That's when I'd been stranded.

I had contemplated going home. After ten minutes of standing against the wall without anyone to talk to and having no clue who to approach, I began heading toward the door. I was planning on texting the girls once I left, just so they knew I was okay. But then, someone stopped me. I felt small looking up at the dark, handsome man with intimidating eyes. His look of arrogance made me feel irrelevant. Then, a softness fell over his features.

"I'm Albert Jefferson," he said.

I didn't know how to reply, realizing that the richest vampire in the world had his hand on my arm. "I'm Anne."

He smiled. "I don't think we've met."

I shook my head.

"Would you like to dance?" Albert asked.

Then, I shook my head and bolted for the door.

Looking back, it had been silly to run from him. But at the time, I had been more intimidated than ever before. At my first ever black-tie event, I'd stuck out and been approached by a charming, billionaire vampire. Now that man was my husband, and it was a strange memory to look back on.

I smiled up at Albert. "Yes, I remember. It was a terrifying evening."

He laughed. "Why? It was just a party."

I raised my eyebrows. "Maybe for you, Mr. Tempting, but not for me. I was petrified."

Albert smirked. "You were so tempted that you ran from me."

I rolled my eyes. "I was embarrassed."

He shook his head. "You shouldn't have been. You were the most beautiful woman in the room. And when you ran from me, I knew you were different. I'd expected you to fall into my arms, but you flew to the door instead. That night changed my life."

I sighed, leaning back against him. "It changed mine,

too."

He laughed. "Then, I had to spend years chasing you."

I laughed. "Yeah, well, if you hadn't been so busy with other women, I would have stopped running."

"Oh really," Albert said.

"Mhm," I murmured.

"Well, maybe you should have said that in reply to one of the dozens of letters I sent you that you never answered," he said.

I bit my lip. "I completely forgot about those."

He rolled his eyes. "I spent hours writing each one."

I reached up, bringing his lips down to mine. "Well, you got me in the end."

Albert smiled. "Yes, I did. And, Mrs. Jefferson, I'll never let you run again."

"Well, Mr. Jefferson, from now on, maybe I'll be the one chasing you," I murmured.

He laughed. "Mhm, I doubt that. Little dove, you're my world. Running away from you would be like falling off the edge of the earth."

He pulled me close, locking our lips together. I let his hands slide up and down my back. He pulled me so tightly against him that I thought I would break, my body simply becoming a part of his. But no, Albert held me with a gentle strength. There was always an edge of love in the tight grip of his hands. He loved me, and I knew it. There was never any doubt that all he did, all he worked for, was Penny and me. It was still a wonder to me that I was actually enough to motivate him. For some reason, this wonderful man loved me. I couldn't explain it. Honestly, it would probably take me many years to fully comprehend it. But still, I knew that, for whatever reason, he loved me. Tangling my fingers in his hair, I lost myself in the maze that is Albert Jefferson.

Chapter Twenty-Six
HAPPINESS

It had been weeks. But finally, the first letters from Nina and Anya had arrived. As soon as the mailman handed them to me, I dashed inside and pulled the first one open.

Dear Anne,

Spain is beyond beautiful. I could never have imagined how gorgeous it would be. The beaches here are lovely, and the sound of the waves is mesmerizing. I could literally lay on the sand all day. They have the most adorable little stores here. And, you'll never guess, we got a puppy! She's a Spanish Pointer, and her name is Rosie. I adore her! I'm sure Penny will love her!

How is Penny? I need pictures, Anne, lots of them. Oh, and I found some adorable dresses for her. I'll mail them to you. But don't forget, I need regular updates on my little niece. She's so big now. I can't believe I'm missing her milestones. But I'm sure she's well taken care of. Albert always hovers.

Now to more serious matters. Like I said, Spain is wonderful. Roy looks happier than he's been since Arthur's death. He smiles regularly, and he's even started learning how to sail. The weather is good for him. He looks young. And Anne, I can't let go of that. He's finally happy. This morning, he told me that he loves it here. I've spoken to a local realtor, who arranged for us to look at a small cottage along the beach. It has beautiful gardens, a little pool, and a boat dock. I can't turn it down, Anne.

I didn't want to tell you this way. We truly were only planning for it to be a trip. Of course, we'll visit. And you have to bring Penny here, she'd love it. I'm not saying we'll never move back to Savannah. Maybe we will, but not soon. For the next few years, I think it would be best for Roy to be away from the place where Arthur died. He talks to Anya every day on the phone. They check in on each other, and every time, I feel my heart begin to break again. Both of their voices adopt a lonely, lost tone. But when he's on the beach and sailing, he smiles. Roy is happy here, so I am too.

We'll visit soon. And, of course, I'll keep writing. Remember, I need pictures of Penny! We have lots of decorating

*to do. You will love the cottage. There's three bedrooms, so
there is plenty of space when you come to visit.*
  With love,
  Nina

I had expected to feel a wave of sadness, but I
didn't. From what Nina said, they were happy in Spain.
That was enough for me to be content with their absence.
Besides, she said they might move back to Savannah.
And we could always visit. If this was the best way for
Nina and Roy to be happy, then it was alright with me.

  Dear Anne,
  *You would love Hawaii. These six months are going to
fly by! There are so many amazing natural wonders. The little
house we're staying in is adorable. And above all, I'm actually
having fun! Nellie is, too. We're both completely in love with
this magical paradise.*
  *How are you doing? Is Albert working too much? Well,
that's hardly a question. I hope you're taking it easy. Really,
you put too much stress on yourself.*
  *There has been another development. I think Nellie is
in love or getting there. She met a gorgeous tour guide. And I
have to say, he really is nice. He's totally into her, too. Being a*

native Hawaiian, he knows all of the best spots. I'll have to call you and tell you more about him.

I'm doing well. It's still hard. Of course, there are moments when I'm able to forget everything. But I still see Arthur in the most beautiful parts of nature. I see him in waterfalls, the ocean, and twinkling stars. I wish he could see all of these wonderful things. But it's getting easier. Every time he crosses my mind, it hurts a little less. I can look back on our relationship with happiness rather than sadness. He was an essential part of my life. But now, I need to move on. And by the time I return to Savannah, I think I'll be a different woman.

Please call soon. I miss you!
Anya

I smiled, a sense of contentment flooding my heart. Anya was getting better, and Nellie was falling in love. Eventually, we would be able to move past the tragedies our family had experienced. Of course, we would never forget James and Arthur. But we may be able to achieve contentment and, eventually, happiness. Yes, we would be alright. Our lives were changing, but not in a bad way. A few years ago, I could have never imagined such a radical change in my life. But now, I'm so glad I stepped out of my comfort zone. It had all led me to Albert.

Things were lining up. Everything was falling into place, allowing for a sense of peace to descend upon us. Finally, there was no enemy to defeat. We didn't have a war to wage or a crazy vampire to control. I no longer had a murderous sister-in-law or a dangerous ex-boyfriend. It was finally time to relax.

Chapter Twenty-Seven
SLIVER OF FOREVER

"How was your day?" Albert whispered.

He placed his hands on my waist, lightly kissing my neck. I smiled into the bathroom mirror as I brushed my hair. He'd been gone all day. For some reason, it had felt like so much longer than nine hours.

"Good, yours?" I asked.

He ran his hand down my back as he moved to stand beside me and remove his suit jacket. "Normal. I had a few disgruntled employees to deal with, but it turned out to just be an HR problem. I handled it."

I shivered. "Doesn't sound fun."

He chuckled. "Well, it wasn't the most enjoyable meeting I've ever sat through. How was Penny?"

I smiled. "She was very imaginative. We read a few books, then I took her to the beach. She kept pointing toward the ocean and saying mermaid over and over again."

He laughed. "Well, it seems like she's been learning something from the fairytales."

"I want to keep her innocent for as long as possible," I said, brushing out the last of my curls.

Albert leaned back against the wall, watching as I adjusted my robe. "She can believe in mermaids and fairies for as long as she wants. After all, she's being raised by two vampires."

I rolled my eyes. "She doesn't know that yet."

He smiled. "Not yet."

I placed my hands on his chest, then leaned up to lightly kiss his lips. He wrapped his arms around my back, reaching to pull me close. His hands tangled in my hair while mine wrapped around his neck. Slowly, I lost all sense of the outside world.

Everything faded away as I became engrossed in him. He overwhelmed my senses, pulling me further and further until I forgot everything else. All I could smell was him, his cologne, and the scent of his cotton suit. I could hear his breathing, the gentle rise and fall of his chest. My eyes were closed, yet I saw stars bloom behind my eyelids as I fell further into his spell. His hands and lips were the only things I could feel as they traveled up and down my back.

In that moment, Albert was all that I could process. He overwhelmed me almost as much as he had the first night we met. That day would forever be present in my mind. Then, of course, there were the years when he'd pursued me, and I'd kept denying my attraction to him. But now, none of that mattered.

Finally, I was in Albert's arms, and we had nothing to run away from. I could finally give him every bit of my love without distraction or stress. We were truly free. The way he kissed me continued to absorb my thoughts. I became unable to form coherent senses, losing all logic to his lips. His body, heart, and soul adored me.

Albert was the greatest love of my life. There was no doubt in my mind that I had found my soulmate. He was the one for me, the most perfect puzzle piece. Every day, he showed me more and more love. Together, we had created our own little family. Albert had given me the life of our dreams. He had made me a queen, a mother, and a wife. And every time his lips touched mine, I felt more and more electricity. I would never become bored of his touch. Albert was just too mesmerizing.

His lips pressed against mine. I felt his fingers pressed more firmly against my skin. His chest rose and fell as his breath became staggered. He was just as overwhelmed by me as I was with him. Albert was like my drug, and I was his. We were intoxicated with each other. Our marriage wasn't dull. It was like fireworks.

"I love you so much, Anne. You're more than I deserve," he mumbled against my lips.

He nuzzled his head against mine. I could barely think. My thoughts were all of him.

"Albert," I whispered, "you're my world. I love you, too."

He pulled me closer, covering my lips with his. I stopped thinking, relishing the feel of his cold, hard wedding ring pressing against my skin. And slowly, we drifted off into our peaceful sliver of forever.

Epilogue

She was graduating from preschool. Penny wore a big, fluffy white dress, sparkly shoes, and white tights. She had a large pink bow in her bright blond curls and a shimmer in her pretty blue eyes. In her tiny hands was a certificate commemorating her graduation from The James Hamilton School For Gifted Children. Albert had founded the school before her second birthday. It was one of his most treasured achievements.

I was always amazed by the school's grand structure. It was a five-story brick building with sprawling gardens, multiple playgrounds, a swimming pool, an indoor greenhouse, a large theater, a huge library, over fifty classrooms, and dorms for higher-level students not local to the area. Inside, the school was magical. With wooden floors and chandeliers, it looked more like Hogwarts than an actual school. The teachers were a mix of vampires and werewolves.

They instructed on everything from English literature to self-defense to Latin and Ancient Hieroglyphics. Albert hired teachers from all around the world, all eager to travel to the only supernatural school in North America. The building was well-kept but not industrial. It was an incredible place. And it was dedicated to James.

Almost all of the children were werewolves. This school was a place where they didn't have to hide who they were. Penny was the singular exception. And soon Azalea, Anya's stepdaughter, would be, too. Anya had married a human man, Carter, whose wife had died, and left him with their baby daughter. Anya and Carter had returned to Savannah and would be sending Azalea to The James Hamilton School For Gifted Children next year.

Nina and Roy were both teachers at the school. Nina taught yoga classes, as well as world history and poetry. Roy did most of the administrative work but also instructed a few courses on inter-pack dynamics, which was required for all the werewolf students.

Penny ran toward me. "See, Mommy! I did it! I graduated!"

I picked her up, planting a kiss on her cheek. "I know. I'm so proud of you!"

Albert pulled both of us into his arms. "You did such a good job, baby. You're going to be as smart as your mommy!"

He took her from my arms, swinging her around, so

her hair flew in the wind. She giggled as he tossed her into the air. My heart always jumped a little when he did that. Penny was so adventurous, so much like Albert. She feared nothing. At only four years old, she already scared me. I had no doubt that she would do wonderful things. But I was also worried that she would get herself hurt. She was wild, impulsive, and sometimes crazy. Still, I loved that about her. She had just as much confidence as her dad and even more sass. Together, they were certainly a challenge.

"Daddy, I wanna play!" Penny shouted, pointing toward the closest playground.

He smiled at her and gently lowered her feet to the ground. "Alright, let's go."

She took off toward the playground, running directly through numerous mud puddles. I sighed, watching as her white dress turned brown. *Oh well,* I thought, *at least it stayed clean for a couple hours.* Yes, she was wild. And I loved it.

Nine Years Later...

"Please, it's just a couple hours. Let me go," Penny asked.

Albert looked up at her with skepticism on his face. His eyes softened as hope crossed her face. I watched the battle of determination, which I was definitely not participating in.

"Hunny, he's three years older than you. I barely know anything about him. But I do know that he's sixteen and has already completed his first transitions. Werewolf boys are so moody at that age. If she gets the slightest bit upset, he could hurt you," Albert replied.

"Just ask Uncle Roy," she said, "Jem is in his inter-pack dynamics class. Uncle Roy loves him."

Albert pursed his lips. "When did you start talking to him?"

"A month ago," Penny answered.

She was very cute in her little blue dress, black sandals, and pink lip gloss. Her blond curls were pulled back in a long braid, and she wore little makeup. With her golden skin and honey hair, she looked like an angel. Her blue eyes pleaded with Albert, urging him to say yes.

Penny was thirteen and entirely crazy about this werewolf boy, Jem. I'd met him once, and he seemed nice enough. But he was three years older than her. Albert was right. Werewolf boys at that age were barely able to control their anger. And I felt odd about sending my thirteen-year-old daughter out with a sixteen-year-old boy. Then again, Albert was far older than me. Still, that was different.

Albert sighed, giving up. "Alright, you can go. But, I want you back from the movie by ten, and he better be a gentleman. If he's not, feel free to tell him I'll rip him limb from limb."

I had to contain my laughter. Penny was grinning like he'd just gifted her a palace. Albert looked irritated, but she didn't seem to mind.

"Thank you," she said, before dashing away to grab her bag.

I walked over to him, placing my hands on his shoulders. "That was entertaining."

He rolled his eyes. "This is terrible."

I laughed. "Albert, it's just one date."

He shook his head. "I should have seen this coming. You know, I could have him expelled."

I raised an eyebrow. "What, so you're just going to expel every boy who talks to her?"

He shrugged. "It does sound appealing."

I began rubbing his back. "We knew she was going to grow up."

"Too soon," he whispered.

I placed a soft kiss against his lips. "I know."

"Okay, I'm ready," Penny said.

She held her little white purse tightly in her hands. Penny looked a little nervous, but not too much. She was probably more scared of what Albert would do than anything that would happen on her date. After all, Albert could be rather…intimidating. I had to admit Jem certainly had some bravery. But he was the son of an alpha. Fear wasn't something he'd grown up around. I was a little surprised he wasn't more interested in a werewolf girl. Hopefully, he wasn't interested in Penny simply because she was unique. I didn't want my daughter to be treated as a challenge. Penny was more than that.

"Where is he?" Albert asked.

"Downstairs," Penny said.

"He came inside a building full of vampires?" Albert asked. "The kid's got guts. Alright, I'm going with you."

Penny smiled before dashing toward the door, and Albert followed.

Albert looked at me. "Are you coming?"

"Oh no, I'm leaving this one to you," I said.

He rolled his eyes. "How kind of you."

I laughed as I watched the elevator door close behind them.

Three Years Later...

"Mom!" Penny screamed as she rushed through the door and slammed it behind her.

I hurried toward her, immediately checking for any signs of injury. "What is it? What's wrong?"

"He left me, Mom!" Penny cried.

My jaw dropped. I could barely believe what I'd just heard. After three years, Jem had left my little girl. Albert might actually kill him. Hopefully not, as that could cause problems. Anger spread through my body as I pulled her tightly against me. Her tears were soaking my shirt as mascara slid down her lashes.

"Why, baby? What happened?" I asked.

She began to cry harder. "He said...he said that his parents didn't want him to be with me because you and Dad are vampires."

"What?" I whispered.

She sobbed against my chest. "He said that he has a duty to his pack, and that means he has to have a son. His parents think I'm not good enough."

I rubbed her back. "Oh baby, I'm so sorry."

"I hate him, Mom. I hate him!" Penny screamed.

I held her tighter, letting her cry until she fell asleep.

~*~

After carrying Penny to her room and putting her in bed, Albert followed me back to our bedroom. Fury was clearly displayed in his eyes.

"What happened? Was it that boy?" Albert asked.

I sighed. "He left her."

"What?" Albert shouted. "He thinks our daughter isn't good enough for him? Well, I'll talk to his parents—"

"Albert," I said, taking his hand in mine, "don't."

He loosened his tie and sat down on our bed. "Why?"

I bit my lip. "This is because of his parents."

Realization crossed his face. "What? They don't want their precious werewolf blood tainted? It's better off she's not with him, then."

I sat down beside him. "Well, I hope so."

He wrapped his arm around me and placed a kiss on my lips. "She'll be alright. I'll find her someone better."

I sighed. "Albert, I don't know."

"Don't worry," he whispered. "There's plenty of better fish in the sea. I'll find someone far better, and then she'll be happy."

I closed my eyes, hoping he was right.

~*~

"Alright, baby," Albert said, "which one do you like?"

Penny looked at him with shock in her eyes. Albert had just handed her three pictures of handsome young men, whom he had definitely done background checks on, to choose from. She held them in front of her, looking at them as though they were some sort of joke.

"If you don't like those, there are plenty more to choose from," Albert said.

He pulled a stack from his pocket, handing them to her. In total, there were probably thirty pictures of werewolf boys, all outstanding in academics and accomplishments. None of them were from the same pack as Jem.

"Dad, I don't want any of them," Penny whispered.

Albert gently touched her hair. "That's alright, baby. I can find more."

She shook her head. "No, Dad. I don't want a boy."

He sighed. "Well, baby, you're not going to get Jem

back."

"I don't care," she said.

It had only been two days since the breakup. She definitely did care. Albert was at a loss. He clearly didn't know how to make her feel better. His inability to do so infuriated him.

"I don't want a boy, Dad," Penny mumbled.

He knelt down in front of her. "What do you want? What would make it better? We can go to London or the Caribbean. I can take a whole month off work. Where would you like to go? We could go shopping in New York City, or I could take you to California. Just pick somewhere."

"I don't want to go anywhere," she whispered.

He looked completely confused. "Well, what do you want?"

Penny looked over at me. She was so devastated. She'd barely eaten anything the past two days. Other than multiple tubs of ice cream, strawberries, smoothies, and iced coffee, she'd refused food. Albert had tried endless tactics, and he was becoming desperate. I barely knew what to do. I'd watched movies with her and listened while she talked, but I couldn't fix it, either. I hated that there was nothing I could do to help her get over him.

Penny made eye contact with each of us. "I want to be a vampire."

Abby Farnsworth is an award-winning Young Adult Paranormal Romance and Fantasy Author. Abby enjoys writing about a wide variety of characters within the Paranormal Romance and Fantasy genres, including faeries, vampires, witches, and werewolves. Her novels are all centered around romance but also feature adventure and suspense. Her first novel, *EverGreen*, received the Literary Titan Silver Star Award, and her second and third novels, *Moonlit Skies* and *Fallen Snow* received the Literary Titan Gold

Star Award.

Abby currently resides in West Virginia and enjoys reading, nature, and long walks.

To learn more about Abby, her books, and her current projects, take a look at the following:
#authorabbyfarnsworth
#theevergreentrilogy
Instagram: @abbyfarnsworth.writer
Facebook: @abbyfarnsworth.writer.poet

www.ingramcontent.com/pod-product-compliance
Lightning Source LLC
Chambersburg PA
CBHW030330180626
46810CB00003B/1298